JOURNEY TO THE CENTER

JOURNEY TO THE CENTER

Brian Stableford

Nelson Doubleday, Inc.
Garden City, New York

Published by arrangement with
DAW Books, Inc.
1633 Broadway
New York, New York 10019

Printed in the United States of America

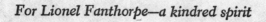

For Lionel Fanthorpe—a kindred spirit

1

If I had had more of a social conscience, events on Asgard might have developed very differently. In fact—or so I have been assured—the ultimate future of the human race may have been affected (for the worse) by my lack of charity. I find this a very sobering thought, and I'm sure there is a moral in it for us all. This is, however, not my purpose in telling the story—I am not in the business of writing moral fables.

Perhaps things would have been different if the call had not arrived in the middle of the night. No one is at his best when summoned from sleep at approximately 12.87 standard metric. I only have a wall phone, which can't be reached from the bed; to answer it I have to wriggle out of the bag and stagger across the room. I usually trip over my boots en route, and this is why I habitually answer the phone with a grunt that sounds more like a curse than a greeting.

The voice that replied to my grunt didn't seem in the least put out. From his cultured tone I tagged him immediately as a Tetron. Pangalactic *parole*, being a Tetron invention, uses a range of phonemes which makes it difficult for anyone *but* a Tetron to speak it in a cultured tone. Humans of western descent always sound barbarous, though the Chinese seem to manage much better. (I speak three Earth languages—English, French and Japanese—but in *parole* I still sound like the interstellar equivalent of a country bumpkin.)

"Am I speaking to Mr. Michael Rousseau?" asked the Tetron.

"Probably," I answered.

"Are you in doubt as to your identity?" he inquired solicitously.

"This is Mike Rousseau," I assured him tiredly. "There's no doubt about it. What do you want?"

"My code is 74-Scarion. I am the officer on duty at Immigration Control. There is a person wishing entry to the city who identifies himself as one of your race. I cannot admit him unless one of his own kind is willing to accept token responsibility for his well-being. As you know, your race has no consulate on this world, and there seem to be no official channels through which I can operate."

"Why me?" I asked, in pained tones. "There must be two hundred humans on Asgard. Or does your version of alphabetical order set my name at the top on your file?"

"Your name was suggested to me by a Mr. Aleksandr Sovorov, who is a member of the Coordinated Research Establishment. I naturally approached him first, believing that he is the one member of your race who is in a position of notional authority. He informed me that he is unable to take responsibility for a person whom he describes as a 'scavenger and fortune-hunter,' and suggested that you would be more likely to have a good deal in common with such an individual."

(As you will note, I am not the only person on Asgard lacking in charity. Far from it, in fact.)

I groaned. "Look," I said, "just what do you expect me to *do* for this character?"

"Simply provide him with a place to stay until he finds accommodation of his own. Familiarize him with the law and with our customs. Act as his host until he is ready to make his own way. That is all."

I was still silently cursing Sovorov, and my reaction was more or less instinctive. "I can't do it," I said firmly. "I'm almost broke. In three or four days—seven at the most—I'm going back out in the cold. In the meantime, I have to get new equipment. I'm not in a position to take in any stray cats."

"I do not understand," replied 74-Scarion. I had to use the English word for cats, of course; there are no such things, I presume, on the Tetron homeworld. The Tetrax don't like us to drop vernacular terms into their carefully molded artificial language. They see it as a kind of pollution. They're probably right.

"I can't do it," I said. "Anyhow, you can't just dump him on the first human that comes to hand. I may not even speak his language. What language *does* he speak?"

In a way, that was getting my own back. There are no words in *parole*, of course, for the human languages. 74-Scarion, however, was unperturbed. A new voice chipped in to answer my question.

"My name is Myrlin, Mr. Rousseau," it said—in English. "I speak English, Russian and Chinese. Not that it matters. I wouldn't want to force myself upon you, if you're unable to accommodate me. I don't want to force myself on anyone, in fact, but the officer here won't admit me to the city unless someone agrees to sponsor me. Is there anyone you can suggest?"

He sounded so polite that I felt guilty. Instead of asking myself whom I disliked enough to visit them with an early-morning phone call I tried to think of someone who'd be in a reasonable position to take care of a stray cat, and who wouldn't mind being asked to do so.

"I think I know someone who can take care of this," I said finally—in *parole*, for the benefit of the Tetron. "There's a man named Saul Lyndrach. He lives in sector six. I met him briefly yesterday. He's just come back from a trip and he seemed quite pleased with the way things had gone. That probably means that he'll be around for a while, and that he's not short of credit. I think he'll be willing to help you out."

"Thank you, Mr. Rousseau," said 74-Scarion smoothly. "I will call Mr. Lyndrach immediately. I'm sorry to have troubled you."

It wasn't until I'd hung up that I began to get curious about Myrlin. I'd been so keen to avoid having him dumped on me that I hadn't asked what he was doing here, or where he'd come from, or any of a dozen other things I might routinely have asked of a fellow human being. After all, when there are fewer than three hundred of one's species in a city of three hundred thousand people, on a world several thousand light-years from Earth, one really should make an effort to be friendly. Poor Myrlin, I thought, would probably figure that every human on Asgard was like Aleksandr Sovorov. I assured myself, though, that Saul Lyndrach would put him right. I resolved to see Saul sometime within the next couple of days, to apologize to him *and* to Myrlin.

That seemed to me to be a reasonable train of thought—just as reasonable, in fact, as the train of thought which had carried me through the telephone conversation. I went back to bed convinced that nothing of any real consequence had occurred.

How was I to know that Mr. so-called Myrlin, who could speak English, Russian and Chinese, was no more human than Mr. 74-Scarion of Immigration Control, and that he might be just about the deadliest menace that our fair species has ever faced?

2

When I got up again, the lights of Skychain City had been burning brightly for some time. It was dark outside the dome, but according to the Tetron timetable it was daytime, and when the Tetron timetable says it's daytime, daytime it has to be. Asgard's own days are about a week long, in Earthly terms —six days Tetron time—but neither we nor the Tetrax could adjust our Circadian rhythms to that kind of regime, so we keep our own time (or, to be strictly accurate, their time). All the other permanent bases on Asgard are on level one, below the surface, but Skychain City has to be on top in order to provide the anchorage for the skychain which shuttles people and goods back and forth from the docking satellite. The satellite and the skychain—and, for that matter, Skychain City itself —are owned by the Tetrax, although the House of Representatives and the police force are multiracial. The joke has it that members of all the humanoid species on Asgard get together to make decisions democratically; they all talk for hours and then decide to do things the Tetron way. That's because the situation is such that if the Tetrax decide not to cooperate, nothing can get done. Such is life.

After breakfast, I went to see my good friend Aleksandr Sovorov. I thanked him kindly for recommending me to the officers of Immigration Control, but what I really wanted to know about was an application I'd put in to C.R.E. for new equipment. I wanted them to hire me the equipment in return for a percentage return on anything I brought back from my expedition into the lower levels. It wasn't a bad deal, from someone with my record, but I wasn't too optimistic about the outcome.

"I haven't had any official notification yet," said Sovorov, rolling a stylo between his short, stained fingers. I could never quite figure out what had stained them. Sometimes I suspect he deliberately dipped them in some kind of reagent, so that he could wear the stains as a badge of office. "I am a scientist," the stains proclaimed. "I work in a laboratory, doing the heavy spadework finding out what all these fancy alien artifacts are made of and how they work." Needless to say, Aleksandr Sovorov thought he was one of the most important men alive. He thought that the future of the human race rested on the shoulders of men like himself.

He didn't know about Myrlin either.

"Did anyone argue the case for me?" I asked. "I mean—is it just a signal flitting from one readout to another, or has someone taken the trouble to go into committee and say: 'Look, lads, this is a good idea. Rousseau is a good man.'? I could do with a little moral support, you know."

Sovorov shrugged. "I don't know of anyone who's prepared to argue your case," he said. "Personally, I wouldn't be prepared to support it. Not that it's my decision, of course."

"You could give me some help if you wanted to. Why won't you?"

Sovorov stabbed at the desk with his stylo, and I wondered what his subconscious was trying to tell me in its sweet, inarticulate way.

"Because," he said, "I don't believe in letting my personal loyalties override my principles. We happen to be members of the same species—we may even be friends—but that doesn't alter the fact that the way you operate has nothing whatsoever in common with the methods and principles of this institution. We are trying to recover the knowledge locked up in the artifacts preserved in the lower levels. We are trying to proceed in a careful and rational manner, one step at a time. We send out our own recovery teams, who are fully trained and whose first priority is safety. They know exactly what they are doing, and they know what to look for. They are not treasure hunters; they are scientists.

"You, by contrast, are a scavenger. You work alone, wandering around aimlessly in unexplored regions, hunting for ways down to new levels, picking up things that take your fancy. Your main aim is not to further the growth of knowledge but to make money by finding objects which have not previously been encountered. God alone knows what damage you do out in the remote regions where you work. If we had our way, scavenging of the kind you indulge in would be outlawed—we would not deal with you and your kind at all if we could have your activities banned. As things stand, we are unfortunately compelled to compete on the open market for many of the prizes which you and others like you bring back to the city. Instead of putting you out of business, we are forced by circumstances to help support you."

"It's a free world," I pointed out (not without a touch of sarcasm). "The Tetrax found it. They could have kept it entirely to themselves. They didn't have to let anyone in. As things stand, I don't see that you're entitled to any special privileges just because you're a multiracial consortium dedicated to advancing the knowledge of a hundred homeworlds instead of an independent operator trying to make a living. No one has any moral title to the stuff that's lying around in the lower levels, except possibly the people way down below, if there are any. We're all parasites, scuttling around the nooks and crannies of Asgard's outer skin, all trying to extract a little profit from our parasitic ventures. You're working for the good of the human race and a hundred other like-minded species—okay, so am I, in my humble way. I'll lay long odds that you've learned a damned sight more from stuff brought in to you from scavengers than from the stuff your own teams have picked up. They're *too* damned orderly and methodical. They don't cover territory the way we do, they pause to look under every last stone. They don't have the intuition we do."

"No doubt they don't travel as far or as fast as you do," said Sovorov. "But from *their* work we are gradually building up a coherent picture of the humanoids who lived on Asgard before the 'big freeze,' as you are so fond of putting it. In time, that solid foundation of knowledge will provide us with the means to discover more and more about Asgard and its technology. In the short term, the fancy gadgets you scavengers bring in might add more to our understanding than the more limited but more coherent information gleaned by our research teams, but in the long run it is our methods which will pay the more handsome dividends. When we are masters of the new technology, you will still be children wandering around in the cold looking for pretty trinkets to pick up. There will come a time when no one will want your trinkets, because we already know everything they have to tell us."

"And when that time comes," said I boldly, "you'll still be scratching the surface. You'll still have gotten no farther than level four. By that time, *my* kind will be halfway down to the center."

He laughed at that. The laughter of the wise when confronted with an unfashionable idea. They laughed at Galileo. They laughed at Christopher Columbus. They also laughed at a lot of cranks, but there's no point in being negative about these things, is there?

If it weren't for positive thinking, we'd never have gotten to Asgard in the first place.

I did have several other irons in the fire, and I spent the rest of the day trying them out to see if any of them had warmed up. As things turned out, none of them had, but I spent a lot of time arguing and haggling before I was finally forced to come to that conclusion.

When no one is prepared to give you what you need, there's really only one thing that you can do, and that's recalculate your needs. There were two ways I could do that. One was to give up operating as a loner and join a team. I could probably hire out to any one of a dozen concerns who kept their field-workers well supplied with adequate life-support systems. The problem with that, of course, was that I'd become a mere employee. If the team I was with made any particularly significant finds, we'd all get some kind of a bonus, but it would be a long way from owning the whole thing myself. I hated to let go of the dream of turning up something really big. It wasn't so much the money that mattered, but the prestige. I wanted people to recognize me when they passed me on the pedwalk. I wanted people on the homeworld I'd never seen to speak my name in awed tones. I wanted to be a hero, a living legend. I'm not altogether sure *why*, but I really did want it badly. It seemed more important than anything else.

The other way I could reduce my needs was by deciding that some of the equipment I already had was good for another trip after all. The returns from my last jaunt had paid for a complete overhaul of my truck, so I was safe to take myself out over the surface to just about any point I cared to pick. The problems would begin when I left the truck and started to go down. My cold-suit could still pass the basic safety checks, but it was getting old and it had taken a lot of wear. The dayside temperature on the surface of Asgard gets high enough to be comfortable, but level one never gets much above freezing point, and level two is a nice, steady hundred and forty below. Down in four it's still only twenty or thirty degrees absolute, just as if Asgard were still in the depths of the dark cloud which—according to Sovorov and his friends in C.R.E.—it had passed through a few million years ago.

Naturally, I wanted to go down to four. I wanted to go down even lower, if I could find a way. If I could find a way, I wanted to go all the way down to the center. Bearing that in mind, going out with anything less than the best equipment was like playing Russian roulette with only one empty chamber. If you're wandering around leaving footprints in oxygen/ nitrogen snow, you can't afford to have your cold-suit develop a fault. You turn into an icicle in a matter of minutes, even if your suit gives out slowly. Rumor has it that if you're ever found, there may be some hope of thawing you out again so that you can take up your life just as you left off, but it's not the kind of gamble a serious student of probability would take. I've seen them try it twice, and each time they ended up with a putrid mess. Even the Tetrax don't have that kind of miracle at their fingertips.

It wasn't just the suit, of course—there was also the matter of supplies. Fuel, gaspacks, food, water—they all had to be bought. The quantity I could buy determined the time I could stay out, and the time I could stay out determined the likelihood of catching something worthwhile. What I had to bear in mind was the fact that if I brought back barely enough to pay my running expenses I'd be even worse off when it came to fixing up the next trip but one. In order to keep the odds in your favor you have to keep on winning. You only have to lose once to be wiped out.

That's why I was trudging around Skychain City looking for a backer instead of heading straight out into the wilderness with every last penny of my credit converted into the necessities of life. I may be a fortune-hunter, in the eyes of a man like Sovorov, but I'm not a fool. I wasn't going to take desperation measures until everyone else on Asgard had turned me down.

My sleep that night was uninterrupted, which was perhaps as well. It was the last decent night's sleep I got for some considerable time. The following morning, Sovorov phoned me to say that my application for an equipment grant had been turned down. He didn't bother to apologize or sympathize. That was before I'd finished breakfast, and I was under the impression that things couldn't get much worse. I was wrong.

I'd just thrown the plates into the grinder when the door buzzer sounded. When I opened the door, I found myself looking at two Spirellans. My immediate instinct was to close the door—not because I have anything against Spirellans as such but because these two were wearing the gaudy clothes that signaled the fact that they were unmated males not yet established in the status hierarchy. The ways in which a Spirellan can win a good place in the status hierarchy of his clan are many and varied, but most of them involve doing someone else down. There are half a hundred races regarded by the Tetrax as being utter barbarians. The human race is one, and the Spirellans are another. Personally, I'd put the Spirellans somewhat lower than ourselves, but I'm biased.

Anyhow, I let them in. In order to get along in a place like Skychain City, where several hundred humanoid races rub shoulders, you have to suppress your instincts.

"My name is Heleb," said the spokesman, his eyes scanning

my room with minute care and patience. "I believe that you are Mike Rousseau." He never once looked at me. I didn't mind that; it meant that he was being polite. When one Spirellan looks directly at another for more than a few seconds it's considered to be a challenge and a threat.

"That's right," I confirmed. He spoke well, but he had an unfair advantage. Spirellans don't look much like Tetrax—they have blue-and-pink marbled skin and two very pronounced skull ridges, which make them look rather like lizards with winged helmets, while the Tetrax look more like moon-faced monkeys with skins like waxed black tree bark—but they have similar mouths, with flat upper palates and protean tongues.

"I hear that you are looking for employment," he said smoothly.

"Not exactly," I told him, eyeing his junior partner suspiciously as he began to pay close attention to the book-tapes stacked in my file-net. The codes were written in English or in French, depending on the display language, so he couldn't read them, but his examination seemed no less intense for that. "I've been trying to raise enough money to outfit a solo expedition. I don't want to sign up with an established team."

Heleb flashed me the Spirellan equivalent of a smile, but his gaze was fixed on a remote spot beyond my shoulder. "I am thinking of mounting an expedition myself," he said. "There would be five of us, including my younger brother Lema." Here he nodded briefly in the direction of his companion. "We have the capital to equip ourselves well, but we do not have an experienced man to assist us. We feel that it would be foolish to set out across the surface without an experienced man. In time, we will be experienced ourselves, but for now we need help. We were recommended to come to you."

"Who by?" I asked.

"An officer of the Coordinated Research Establishment. He knew that your application for an equipment grant had just been turned down, and he wanted to help you."

"He must have known before I did," I muttered. To Heleb, I said: "I'll have to think it over."

There are some races—or, at least, some classes of persons within certain races—who don't recognize the propriety of a diplomatic refusal. They're apt to take it as an insult.

Heleb looked me in the eye just long enough to let me know that he wasn't pleased.

"I have invited you to join me," he said, levelly. "Your hesitation might be considered an insult."

"No insult is intended," I assured him, making sure I didn't look too long at *him*.

"I think that you should accept my invitation," he said.

"I still have several alternatives open to me," I assured him, lying in my teeth. "I will consider them all."

"Make sure that you consider carefully," he said. Then, abruptly, he signaled to his brother, who was still taking an altogether unwarranted interest in my reading material, and they left, closing the door quietly behind them.

I sat down on the bed and wondered what fate had against me. The last thing I needed was to get into a quarrel with a Spirellan just because some idiot at C.R.E. had convinced him that I was the man he needed to make his first adventure in the cold country a successful one. If Heleb really believed that, then he would put pressure on—Spirellans set a lot of store by success.

I felt in desperate need of a sympathetic ear and some moral support, so I decided to go see Saul Lyndrach, and get a look at mysterious Myrlin at the same time.

Unfortunately, Lyndrach wasn't home. Like me, he lived in a one-room cell in a honeycomb singlestack—one of a couple of hundred erected by the Tetrax when they first built the base that had expanded into Skychain City. The building supervisor hadn't seen him go out, and hadn't seen him at all since noon the previous day, when he'd passed through in the company of a giant. The giant (he assured me solemnly) had been a good head taller than Lyndrach, who was himself a head taller than me. That didn't sound likely. Lyndrach was nearly two meters tall, and that was big by the standards of ninety-eight per cent of the humanoid races foregathered on Asgard. If the giant was

Myrlin, then he was a pretty exceptional human being—I thought.

I went down to Lyndrach's local drinking den, knowing that he spent a lot of time there. It seemed more likely that he'd be there, telling his visitor all his weird ideas about Asgard and the center and the missing indigenes, than that he'd be showing the newcomer the sights of Skychain City.

The bartender told me that Saul hadn't been in all day, and that he hadn't brought any giants in at any time. I nearly let it go at that, but thought I might as well stay for a quick drink. While I sipped it, another thought occurred to me.

"Hey," I said to the bartender—A Zabaran, I think—"do you know a Spirellan called Heleb? Has a brother called Lema."

It was an innocent question, I thought, but the bartender moved back a couple of paces.

"What if I do?" he countered.

I frowned, not having expected the guarded reaction.

"What's wrong with him?" I asked suspiciously.

"It's none of my business," said the Zabaran.

"Whose business is it?" I inquired, feeling more anxious by the moment.

As he turned away to attend to another customer, the bartender muttered: "Guur." To the uninitiated, it would have been a meaningless grunt, but to me it was a name. Amara Guur—a Vormyran. Not a nice person—rather the opposite, in fact.

Heleb had been worrying me sufficiently on his own. If he was really working for Amara Guur, then the import of his visit might be considerably worse than I'd imagined. I could think of no reason whatsoever why Amara Guur might be interested in me, but if there was a reason, it was unlikely to be one that might work to my advantage. *Extremely* unlikely.

As I continued to sip my drink, I began to think that the best possible thing I could do might be to get out of Skychain City without waiting for lights out. A sense of urgency the like of which I had never felt before began to impress itself upon me, and I didn't like it. I might well have yielded to that impulse, in which case this would have been a much shorter and simpler story, but my attention was distracted by the arrival of another of my fellow humans—one who, like Saul Lyndrach, was in the same line of business as myself. His name was Simeon Balidar.

Truth to tell, I didn't like Balidar much. Maybe I had too much in common with him. He was always hunting for information about profitable hunting grounds. We all were, of course, except that Balidar would rather spend three weeks picking up hints about someone else's finds than two weeks making a find of his own. He really *was* a scavenger, following where others led in the hope of profiting by their efforts. In spite of all this, though, I never tried to avoid him and I never picked a quarrel with him. No matter how long you live among aliens, or how close you get to members of other species, you still remain dependent on the nearness of your own kind. That's why Aleksandr Sovorov, no matter how fiercely he disapproved of me, would still say, sincerely, that I was his friend. No matter how misanthropic a man might be (and he probably wouldn't be a starman if he wasn't), he keeps up appearances with other members of the human race. Those appearances are worth something.

Balidar greeted me as if there were no one else in the world he'd rather see. I asked him about Saul Lyndrach, but he was no wiser than I. We talked for a while, to no good purpose—I didn't have any secrets that I didn't mind giving away—and eventually we joined a game of cards that was going on in one of the back rooms. My main motive for doing so was to alleviate the growing tedium of our conversation. It gave me something to do to take my mind off the disturbing uncertainties of my predicament.

Two of the other players were Zabaran, the other was a Sleath. Balidar obviously knew them, and they all claimed to know Saul Lyndrach, though none of them had seen him or knew anything about his whereabouts. They had heard no rumors of giants, either—or so they said.

I hadn't much spare credit, and I resolved to leave after I'd lost the very modest investment that I initially put into the game. I expected to lose—we were playing a Zabaran game which was simple enough in principle but complicated enough to give regular and practiced players a significant advantage.

As things turned out, however, I began to win. Skill had nothing to do with it; I was simply fortunate with the cards.

Time after time, I was favored by the fall, and the Sleath, in particular, began to get upset about it. For one thing, he was the big loser, and for another, he really wasn't doing anything wrong. He was playing the odds quite sensibly—he simply kept getting beaten. That's enough to try the patience of a saint. By the time I had eleven or twelve times my original investment piled up in front of me, I was getting quite embarrassed—not that I was about to give any of it back. I could tell that the Sleath was beginning to wonder whether I was cheating, and I was glad that most of my wins were coming up on other people's deals. Balidar made a couple of cracks about my good fortune that could easily be taken two ways, but I couldn't see that the Sleath had any excuse to get upset except for the fact that he hated losing. Who doesn't?

Some people play more cautiously when they're losing. Others play more aggressively. The Sleath was one of the latter kind. He began betting more often, raising the stakes when he could. That only increased the probability that he would continue losing, and he did.

I knew that some kind of bust-up was inevitable half an hour before it happened. It didn't particularly worry me. It was up to the Zabarans to stop their friend from doing anything stupid, and if they were too slow I ought to have no difficulty in handling a Sleath. In all probability he'd never seen his home-world—no more had I—but he carried its heritage in his genes. He was thin and light, adapted for fast movement in an environment where the gravity was four-fifths of what it is on Asgard. In order to get around on Asgard he needed to wear supportive clothing—he was dressed in what was effectively an artificial exoskeleton. He couldn't afford to get into any fights, especially not against someone whose physique—by coincidence —was more or less perfectly adapted for Asgardian conditions.

His temper gave out when he lost a hand to me that virtually wiped him out. It was mostly his own fault—he'd played it with as much subtlety as a man in a cold-suit trying to dance a jig—but he turned to the Zabarans and pointed an accusing finger at Balidar, who'd dealt the hand.

"They're cheating us!" he said. "Don't you see—they're working as a team. Balidar's been throwing his friend perfect cards all day."

The Zabarans each referred to the stacks of chips in front of them. They were both losing, but hardly enough to pay for a round of drinks. Balidar was losing more than the pair of them put together.

"Look," I said amiably, "the cards haven't done you any favors, but you haven't exactly shown them the respect they deserve. If you calm down, you'd probably play better."

"You bastard!" he said (or words to that effect), and pulled a knife.

I moved away from my chair, picking it up as I did so. By the time he was within striking range, I had the chair in front of me. When he lunged, I clipped his wrist with one leg and rammed the opposite one into his left eye. The howl he let out had so much more rage in it than pain I thought that discretion demanded further action. I hit him over the head just hard enough to make him collapse.

The door behind me had opened, and I turned around, expecting the space to be filled with inquisitive faces.

There were faces all right, but they didn't look particularly inquisitive. They were, however, familiar. One of them belonged to the bartender, but the other two were both Spirellans: Heleb and his little brother.

I was still holding the chair, and any thought I'd had of putting it down was now gone. I looked at Balidar, expecting moral support. He was looking at the ceiling, absentmindedly shuffling the cards.

Heleb was looking at me, hard and steady. He didn't say a word. He didn't have to.

"Hello, Heleb," I said, as casually as I could. "Are you looking for me?" To one of the Zabarans I said: "Cash me those chips, will you."

The Zabaran made no move to comply. The bartender closed the door, leaving Heleb and Lema on the inside. It felt rather as if I were alone.

The room had no window, and Tetron glass doesn't shatter anyway. If I was going to get out, I was going to have to go past Heleb—or more likely over him.

"The trouble with humans," said Heleb, in his neatly pronounced *parole*, "is that they're barbarians. They're vicious, and they have no respect for the customs of other races. They have no concept of honor."

I couldn't help glancing at Balidar again, but he was still avoiding my gaze. Some humans, it seemed, definitely *were* lacking something. He'd set me up.

"You cannot get away with murder," Heleb continued. "Not here. There is law here, and the law has to be observed. How else can we all live together?"

He was still staring at me, but he hadn't made a move to *do* anything.

The Sleath rolled over, making an audible groan. So much, I thought, for murder.

"Cash those chips!" I said, my voice harsh. This time, the Zabaran banker moved, and began to count the chips. He took his time, and in the meantime the rest of us might have been frozen solid. There was no sound but the clicking of the counters, and then the rustle of the Tetron credit notes which were the official trade medium of Skychain City.

By the time I turned to pick up the cash, however, the Sleath was very much alive again. He was sitting up, and when he saw me reach out for the money, he went for his knife again. It was lying on the floor, near the table leg, and I had no difficulty stamping on his fingers as he reached for it.

That was when Heleb moved.

Fighting a Spirellan is a very different matter from fighting a Sleath. Heleb was as well adapted to the gravity as I was, and he was trained in unarmed combat of the type practiced by his people. But the chair was still in my left hand, and I lashed out with all the force I could muster. He was expecting it—not unnaturally—and he rolled with the blow, getting a good two-handed grip on the chair himself. He added his own strength to the force of my blow, and if I hadn't let go I'd have ended up doing a somersault into the wall.

With the credit notes in my right fist, I dived for the door. Heleb tripped me, and little brother Lema delivered a neat chop to the back of my neck. I went down on to my knees, dazed but still conscious, and tried to lunge forward again. My shoulder ran into the closed door, which didn't budge an inch. Stiff fingers closed on the sides of my neck, groping for the carotid arteries.

Someone, I thought as I passed out, has been doing research on human anatomy.

5

I woke up with a terrible hangover, reeking of some aromatic liquor from God-knows-where. I thought it was a little odd, but it took me several seconds to remember that I hadn't been drinking at all, let alone stinking like garbage that was enough to make a sensitive man vomit.

I opened my eyes and was instantly dazzled by the bright light. I had to blink furiously a dozen times before I could stand it. When I finally managed to look around, I found that I was in a cell. It was spotlessly clean, and one of its four walls was made of clear glass. The glass sparkled with flashes of reflected light. There was no mistaking the Tetron handiwork.

I rolled off the low-slung bunk, and tried to stand up. At the third attempt, I managed it. The glass wall was solid except for a mesh panel at about head height, where there was an incoming current of fresh air. I took of couple of deep breaths, and then banged with my fist on the glass. A couple of minutes passed before the guard appeared. He was a Tetron, of course, dressed like any other Tetron civil servant.

"What time is it?" I asked.

"Thirty-two ninety," he replied.

That meant I'd slept all night.

"How did I get here?"

"The police brought you."

"Where from?"

"I'm not sure. Would you like me to look at the arresting officer's report on you?" His tone was gentle and concerned, unfailingly polite.

"Don't bother," I said. "Can you remember what the charges were?"

"Murder," he replied. "It is alleged that you killed a Sleath by battering him to death."

I groaned. I didn't bother to say: "It's a lie!" or "I was

framed." It wouldn't make any difference. He would simply have reminded me that as I was to be presumed innocent until proven guilty I could be sure that he personally would maintain an open mind on the question.

"Can you find me a lawyer?" I said to him.

"Certainly," he said. "Did you have any particular lawyer in mind?"

"I don't know any," I said. "Could you call Aleksandr Sovorov at the Coordinated Research Establishment and ask his advice? He's certain to know a dozen."

"I will do that," promised the guard. "Is there anyone else you would like me to notify?"

"Yes," I said. "A man named Saul Lyndrach. Ask him to come to see me. I'm going to need all the help I can get. Can you get me some water to drink?"

"Of course. Would you like some food also?"

"Not just now. But I could do with getting rid of the stink of whatever foul stuff they forced down my throat after they knocked me out."

"There is a shower-bath behind the rear partition. There is also apparatus for cleaning clothes. Do you need instruction on the operation of these fitments?"

I shook my head wearily.

He went away. Tetron penology really is based on the highest ethical conduct—they say. Their treatment of criminals is supposed to be the most enlightened in the galaxy. A Tetron jail is just about the nicest place there is to be held for trial. The only trouble is, no one gets to stay in one for more than a couple of days. They don't use them for convicted criminals.

By the time I'd had a drink of water, washed myself and cleaned my clothes, I was feeling a great deal better. The only trouble was that the better I felt, the better I was able to appreciate the enormity of my situation. I was in a very deep hole. Obviously, nothing that had happened to me the previous day had happened by chance. Heleb and Balidar were both part of some kind of conspiracy, whose purpose was to frame me for murder. And behind it all, if the grunting bartender had meant what he seemed to say, was Amara Guur. Why Amara Guur should have the slightest interest in me was beyond my comprehension, but I knew only too well that any interest he did have was extremely unlikely to work out to anything but my ultimate disadvantage. Too many of the people Amara Guur took an interest in wound up dead.

My lawyer turned up at forty-one ten, full of apologies about being delayed. He explained, regretfully, that it had proved impossible to contact Saul Lyndrach, who had, apparently, disappeared. He was, of course, entitled to disappear if he wanted to, but the Tetrax were looking for him because they were anxious about a human named Myrlin, for whom he had accepted responsibility.

The lawyer's name was 238-Zenatta. He was, of course, a Tetron.

"The evidence for the prosecution is all on file already," he told me. "It merely remains for me to prepare your defense. Naturally, I will need your full cooperation in this matter, but it seems to me that your only chance to minimize the magnitude of the offense is to plead diminished responsibility due to alcoholic poisoning."

"Like hell it is," I told him. "I didn't do it!"

"I'm so sorry," he said. "I hadn't realized that there might be a dispute. Please explain in your own words exactly what did happen."

I gave him a blow-by-blow account of the whole sequence of events. I explained my conspiracy theory.

"This account differs rather markedly from the account agreed on by all the other witnesses," said 238-Zenatta, in the Tetron equivalent of an anxious tone. "Simeon Balidar has admitted that you and he were, in fact, cheating. The cards used in the game have been deposited as evidence, and have been shown to be marked by strategically placed grease stains. Balidar agrees with the two other players, and with the Spirellans, that the blows which you gave the dead man were, indeed, the cause of his fractured skull. There is no mention in their testimony of a knife. Actual bodily harm was also suffered by the man Heleb, and a substantial amount of damage done to the property where the affray took place. The prosecution has established that you have spent some time attempting to raise money to furnish equipment for an exploratory expedition into the lower levels, and that you refused Heleb's offer of employment, telling him that you had another way of raising capital.

It is suggested that the only thing to which you could have been referring was your intention to make money cheating at cards, assisted by Simeon Balidar. Balidar confirms this. It would be extremely difficult to attack this testimony in any way. There seems to be no obvious point of weakness."

"There wouldn't be," I said hollowly. "It's a carefully constructed edifice of lies. Someone has taken a lot of trouble to build it."

"But Mr. Rousseau, why should they? Why should anyone go to the lengths of committing a murder in order to have you convicted of the crime? If there has been a conspiracy, there must have been a reason for it. What is it?"

That, of course, was the big question. Without an answer to that, not even the most charitable and trusting Tetron in the galaxy could begin to believe me.

"Could you establish a link between Balidar and Heleb? Suppose we could demonstrate that they were all tied in with Amara Guur, one way or another?"

The Tetron shook his head. "Perhaps we could. What would it prove? To demonstrate the existence of a conspiracy one needs far more than evidence of the fact that a set of witnesses have acquaintances in common. I repeat, why should Amara Guur—or anyone else—want to have you convicted of murder?"

"Well," I said, thinking as rapidly as I was able. "It's nothing I've done to *him*. There's no reason anyone would want revenge for anything I've done. So, if the reason isn't in the past, it must be in the future. Guur has to be trying to take advantage of your cockeyed penological system. He wants to buy my services."

The Tetrax, of course, are as enlightened in their treatment of convicted criminals as they are in their treatment of the accused-but-not-yet-convicted. So they say. Effectively, all crimes represent debts to society which have to be repaid. Specifically, they represent debts payable to the parties injured by the crime. In the case of death, the claimants are the dependants of the victim—his family, his employer, and so on. If I were to be convicted, the court would decide what reparation I would have to make, depending on my circumstances. There was no fixed fine for murder—that would effectively allow men who were rich enough to get away with it. It would automatically cost me all the credit I had and more. The "more" would have to be earned. I could work for the Tetrax, doing something that could well turn out to be hard and disagreeable, at a rate of pay which *they* would set. They would have paid off the full amount of my calculated debt, and in working for them I'd have to work off that sum *and* the interest (again at a rate *they* set).

On Earth we have a word for that; it's called slavery. The Tetron equivalent doesn't carry quite the same emotional overtones. The alternative to working for the Tetrax is to become a bonded slave for someone else—anyone, in fact, who will offer a contract for your services. The contracts have to comply with certain standards—even slaves have rights with respect to their treatment—but they're fairly flexible. Anyhow, if I were convicted I'd have the option of accepting an offer from an outside source to pay off the whole of my debt immediately in return for a specific number of days (or, more likely, years) of some specific kind of service.

There is yet another alternative—in theory, at least—and that is refusal to cooperate. No one can make you work at anything if you say no. That's when the gloves come off. What happens then is that the Tetrax put you into a coma, and use your body as a factory producing various organic compounds, and even live viruses. If you don't work as a man, you work as a machine. That takes longer still, and when you've served your term, you tend to be not quite the man you once were. Not many people take that option, though some races which have peculiar metabolic systems are so much in demand that they can actually get off with much shorter sentences that way.

Anyhow, the implications of all this are easy enough to see: if you're a particularly nasty-minded person, and you particularly want to obtain the services of some other person, you might consider framing him for a particularly nasty crime, and then offering him a moderately favorable bond contract, knowing that the alternatives which face him are likely to be far less attractive. Of course, if he realizes that you framed him, he's likely to spit in your eye regardless, but he has to be pretty stubborn if the Tetrax are demanding twenty years of his life and you're only asking two.

"But I don't see," said 238-Zenatta, "why Amara Guur

should *want* to acquire your services. There are hundreds of scavengers in Skychain City. Why would he want *you?*"

That, of course, was the big problem. It was a great theory, if only I could figure out some reason why Amara Guur might want *me* badly enough to set up a murder in order to catch me.

It didn't seem to make much sense.

I could tell just by looking that 238-Zenatta didn't think it made any sense at all. He might be too polite to say so, but in his heart of hearts he was one hundred percent convinced that I was guilty as hell.

Who could blame him?

"Slavery," I said, "is an abomination. No civilized society should tolerate it."

I'd just watched my trial on television. 238-Zenatta had put up what seemed to me to be a rather lackluster performance, but I couldn't really believe that anyone else would have done any better. The magistrate, needless to say, had found me guilty. My appeal had been dismissed in a matter of minutes. Now I was waiting out the statutory three days when someone might offer to buy me out. I was playing cards with my jailer, whose name was 69-Aquila. He had not made a single crack about marked cards. Mind you, they were his cards and he was winning. We were playing a game of skill without the involvement of money.

"How do you treat criminals on your homeworld?" he asked.

I told him.

He laughed.

"I realize, of course, that *everything* we lesser species do seems to you to be barbaric," I said. "But you must be able to understand that sometimes the reverse seems to be true. To us, some of your customs seem barbaric. We abandoned slavery more than four hundred years ago."

"That only serves to demonstrate how backward your culture is," he answered. "There are a great many things that you *could* have given up whose abandonment would testify to a certain level of enlightenment. War, for instance. I understand, however, that far from giving it up, your species has actually been engaged in an interplanetary war for almost all the time span during which you have been using starships."

"So it's rumored," I conceded, "but you're changing the subject. It's *your* conduct that's in question, not ours. I am sitting here waiting for someone to offer to buy me. If they don't, I will automatically be forced to work for you in whatever capacity you find convenient—either that or have myself turned into a laboratory animal with my mind switched off for the next twenty years. I find this a rather invidious position to be in. I don't think anyone should be subjected to this kind of treatment."

69-Aquila shrugged. "It is necessary," he said. "In fact, it is not merely necessary, but inevitable. The Tetrax have had the opportunity to study the historical development of thousands of humanoid cultures. There is a pattern in these data which our scientists have analyzed and explained. The kind of social relationships which exist in a humanoid culture depend very largely on the technology which the culture possesses. As technology develops, so the economic basis of their existence changes. In the beginning, when there is no technology to speak of, and all of every man's labors are devoted to the business of survival, there is no complex social organization. The main social groups are families or tribes; political power is simply brute force.

"When knowledge has advanced sufficiently to allow a relatively small number of agricultural laborers to produce food enough to feed twice their number, cities can grow, and with them more complicated organizations. Political power is entirely bound up with control of the land, because those who control the land control the food surpluses which the land produces, and this is what sustains the city dwellers.

"When knowledge has advanced still further, a more complex technology emerges, and machines begin to take over much of the business of production. Agriculture becomes even more efficient, and cities expand. Factories appear, and the men who control the machines enjoy growing political power which enables them to compete with the men who enjoy power by virtue of controlling the land. This is the stage of history which your own culture is currently experiencing. Naturally, it seems to you to be the end of the sequence. If you had imagination, though, you would understand that it is not; but instead you preoccupy yourselves with endless squabbles about which individuals should control the land and the machines, or which political institutions should take them over.

"We know the pattern of history as it extends beyond your barbaric phase, though you will not listen to us when we explain it to you. Really, it is obvious, but barbarians are notoriously stupid and illogical. What will emerge from your present cultural condition—and probably is emerging even now, if only you had eyes to see—is a new system of social relationships. Just as feudalism was replaced by capitalism, so capitalism will be replaced by slavery. It is inevitable. Your technology is even now elaborated to the point where the provision of almost unlimited energy is feasible. Once you mastered the frame force and found the way to travel between the stars, the matter of land control ceased to be of any real importance—though your stupid territorial war against your barbaric neighbors shows that you have failed to understand this. Similarly, you now have the mechanical power to overproduce your needs —you live in an economy of abundance. For all I know, there may still be people starving on your homeworld, but if so, it is unnecessary, and in any case there are no people starving on any world managed by the Tetrax. Control of machines has therefore ceased to be a crucial source of political power.

"So, what is the crucial source of political power? I will tell you—it is the control of other people; the control of the services which they can perform for one another. In truth, this was always the crucial element in political power—it is political power—but in the primitive stages of social history it is an end achieved indirectly, by the application of intermediate means. In the final phase, there are no more intervening means; the end is achieved directly. All social relationships begin to take the form of institutions which function by giving one man control over the services of another. Money comes to symbolize labor rather than commodities, and any obligations incurred by members of society—whether they are voluntary or involuntary —have to be discharged through contracts of service. In an economy of abundance, how else can a man discharge a debt save by selling *himself*? He has nothing else to sell. Call it 'slavery' if you wish, but that will not make it any less inevitable. It is the destiny of all humanoid societies."

"It's a fascinating theory," I said. "But it doesn't make me feel any better about things."

"We call it the theory of dialectical materialism," said 69-Aquila, as he totted up the points in yet another game.

"I think we had something similar on my homeworld," I said.

He laughed. "How ridiculous you barbarians are!" he replied. "You are all the same. We tell you our discoveries, and if you do not deny them you try to claim that you already know them. Don't you see how absurd you are? Only by the painstaking comparison of the histories of countless humanoid races could anyone induce any empirical generalization of this sort. How *could* you produce such a theory without having the opportunity to observe that which is common to hundreds of different cases?"

"I still say that it's a violation of my rights as a sentient being to put me in a position where I'm forced to sell myself to the lowest bidder," I said, retreating back to my original position. You can't win an argument with a Tetron. It just isn't possible.

"There you go again," said 69-Aquila. "If you can't claim the theory for your own you just don't want to understand it. Willful stupidity, that's all it is. If you think we're so uncivilized, perhaps you'd rather the vormyr were running things here?"

"The vormyr bloody well *are* running things here," I told him (though I had to add the swear words in my own language—pangalactic *parole* doesn't have any). "You may run the legal system, but Amara Guur runs organized crime. You caught, tried and convicted me, but Amara Guur set me up. You're just the means—his are the ends. *That's* what I'm complaining about."

This time, at least, he had the grace not to laugh. He just let the remark go by, refusing to take it seriously.

"I hope you don't mind my asking," I said, "but there's one thing about you Tetrax I've never quite understood. Why is it that you have code numbers instead of names?"

Sometimes you have to be wary of asking aliens personal questions of that kind. You're apt to give mortal offense by making out that their most sacred customs are screwy. The Tetrax, though, are very hard to offend.

"We use numbers as identifiers for precisely the opposite reason that most races refuse to be numbered and insist on names," he answered levelly. "You refuse to be numbered because you are afraid of losing your individuality, anxious lest you become an insignificant unit in a larger social whole. By 'become,' of course, I mean 'become in your own estimation.' We refuse to be named because we are afraid of losing our collectiveness, our membership of a larger whole, anxious lest we become insignificant individuals divorced from our context of meaning. Again, 'become' means 'become in our own estimation.' It is all a question of how we interpret our situation—the objective features of the situation hardly matter, in that we are always individuals *and* members of a group within our particular species. Do you see?"

"It sounds crazy to me," I told him.

"That," he said, "is what reassures me in moments of existential crisis that after all we must be sane. It is when you begin to agree with us that we begin to worry."

As I said, you can't win an argument against a Tetron.

Our uplifting conversation was interrupted at that point by an incoming signal on his wristphone. He consulted the display and then looked up at me.

"It seems," he said, "that someone wishes to offer you a contract."

"Fancy that!" I replied.

I wasn't expecting Amara Guur in person, of course. I half expected Heleb, who had already tried to purchase my services in a more orthodox fashion, but a moment's thought would have assured me that having been one of the witnesses at my trial he'd be kept out of the picture for a while.

The person who actually did appear, to make me the offer I supposedly couldn't refuse, was a woman named Jacinthe Siani. She was a Kythnan.

All the humanoid races of the galactic community are more or less similar, in that they all have two legs, two arms, one head and some way of exchanging fairly sensible communication. That still leaves a lot of leeway, however, for the eccentric arrangement of sense organs, skin type, etc., etc. There are various systems of classification reflecting different priorities of similarity and difference, but on a crude level one can say that there are maybe half a dozen alien species so similar to humankind that it wouldn't seem perverted to screw their women. Kythnans belong to that small but select category. (I shall refrain from making any jokes about Kythnan and kin.)

Jacinthe Siani was sufficiently beautiful to make the thought of screwing her not merely tolerable but extremely attractive. She had a sort of faint greenish tinge, but apart from that she could have passed for a Balinese. She didn't have pointed ears, though. I really like pointed ears.

"As time goes by," I said to her, "my situation comes to seem more and more surreal. Amara Guur is really going to a lot of trouble, isn't he? First Heleb and the iron fist; now you and the velvet glove. He's overdoing it, you know."

"I don't know what you're talking about," she purred. She had a soft, low voice that sounded very nice.

"No," I said, "I don't suppose you do. Let me guess, now—you're the recruiting officer for your local stud farm?"

"I need a man with your expertise," she said.

"Precisely," I replied.

"Your expertise in lower-level exploration," she elaborated.

"Oh," I said, trying to sound surprised and disappointed. It wasn't the best line I'd ever delivered. To tell the truth, I wasn't really up to a lengthy exchange of merry banter.

"The people I represent," she went on, "are mounting an expedition which will penetrate farther into the core than any previous one. We intend to look for a route down to the center."

"I know just the man you want," I said. "He knows more

about the center than any other man on Asgard. It's almost an obsession with him. Name of Saul Lyndrach."

For just a fleeting moment, a shadow crossed her face. Her eyes narrowed, and there was more than surprise in the brief frown. I hadn't expected any reaction at all. I was just making conversation.

"Hey," I said. "There's a guilty secret somewhere around here. What's Lyndrach got to do with this? You wouldn't have anything to do with his sudden disappearance, would you? How about a big man named Myrlin—do you know him?"

There was no reaction to any of that. I no longer had the advantage of surprise.

"I'm prepared to offer you a two-year contract," she said. "You'll have the customary protection against physical abuse and measurable hazard."

"Sure," I said. "Once we're out in the cold, all the safety clauses would be worth as much as a spoonful of nitrogen snow."

"Don't be a fool," she said. "It's your expertise we need. It's in our interests to make sure you stay healthy."

"Absolutely," I agreed. "It's what happens when I'm no longer needed that worries me. Why me, anyhow? Skychain City is crawling with treasure hunters of half a hundred different species, and two in three have logged more cold time than I have. What's so special about poor Mike Rousseau?"

"You're available," she pointed out.

"But I'm not cheap," I countered. "You have to buy me off a murder rap. You could buy a dozen men for less than that. You could probably have just about anyone you wanted, except perhaps Saul Lyndrach. If you'd wanted him, you'd have had to do more than frame him for the murder of some poor benighted Sleath. But you know that, don't you? You've already tried Saul. What is it about humans that you find so attractive?"

"I like to work with people I can be at ease with," she said. "You're as close to my own kind as the product of an alien creation could be."

"Yeah," I said. "I've learned a lot about the mysterious workings of the long arm of coincidence these last few days. There's another guy I could recommend if you want someone *really* cheap. He goes by the name of Simeon Balidar. But then, he's already one of the gang, isn't he?"

"I've never heard of him," she said. She seemed to have had a lot of practice telling blatant lies. "In any case, I want you."

"How flattering," I muttered. The way she said it made it sound attractive. But then, bait always *is* attractive, isn't it?

"It's a good contract," she assured me. "What alternative do you have?"

"I could work for the Tetrax."

"For half a lifetime?"

"It's not much," I agreed, "but it's a living. I'd have job security."

"I wouldn't bank on that," she said. "Some of the work the Tetrax offer to their charges is pretty hazardous. You might not live out the first year of your sentence."

Her tone was casually neutral, but I know a threat when I hear one.

"You really are taking a lot of trouble, aren't you?" I said.

"We don't mind taking trouble," she assured me, "in order to get what we want."

"It's always possible that I'll get another offer," I pointed out. "After all, if my reputation is as high as you think, there might be a dozen outfits trying to buy my services."

"I don't think so," she said. "In fact, I'd be astonished if you were to receive another offer."

"I don't care how astonished you'd be," I told her. "The law gives me three days, and I'm going to take advantage of it. After the time's up, maybe I'll sign your lousy contract. Amara Guur holds all the cards in the pack, for the moment, but I'm not going to make it any easier for him to play them. You tell him that. I'll see you again when the deadline expires—until then. . . ."

I left it at that; there was nothing else I could say that wouldn't sound absurd.

She smiled. "You can call anyone you like," she said, "but no one's going to buy you out. You don't have any friends with that kind of credit. In fact, I'll be surprised if you can dig up any friends at all."

So saying, she left. I kicked the glass wall, but all that got me was an aching toe.

I had a dreadful suspicion that she was right.

The first person I tried to call, not unnaturally, was Saul Lyndrach. He wasn't home. I called 74-Scarion at Immigration Control to ask if he knew anything of Myrlin's whereabouts, but he didn't. He admitted to some faint concern, but also said that no actual investigation was being conducted. As far as he was concerned, it seemed, once Saul had accepted responsibility for Myrlin, Immigration Control had washed their hands of him.

Where else was I to turn for help?

I tried Aleksandr Sovorov, not feeling particularly confident.

"Alex," I said earnestly, "I didn't do it."

"Actually," he replied, "I didn't really think you had."

"I was framed. By Amara Guur. Crazy as it may seem, he seems to be backing some kind of expedition into the lower levels."

"Crazy as it may seem," he agreed, "he seems to be doing exactly that. Rumors whirl around this place fairly quickly, as you'll understand. All those silly stories about the center are back in circulation. It happens about once a year, in my experience, but this is the first time that the vormyr have fallen for it. The mysteries of Asgard get to us all in the end, I suppose."

"Get me out," I said, not wishing to indulge in a philosophical debate about the mind-bending effects of popular mythology.

"I'd like to help," said Sovorov, "but I don't really see how I can. I don't have any money."

"The C.R.E. has funds. I'll sell them my services on any terms they care to name. Ten years—even fifteen. Just get me out."

"The C.R.E. doesn't operate like that," he informed me.

"Alex," I said, patiently, "this is a matter of life and death.

Okay, so you didn't feel that you could lend your support to my application for an equipment grant. I can understand that. But this is different. I don't care what C.R.E. policy is, I want you to get off your fat ass and start changing it. You have got to help me get out of this."

"Mike, you just don't understand," he told me—not, I might add, for the first time. "The Coordinated Research Establishment is a very special institution. People from dozens of different races pooling their resources, their knowledge, their efforts, to work toward a collective goal. You've no idea how difficult that is—how delicate is the balance we have to maintain. Everyone here, no matter what his species, has to put his personal, insular loyalties to one side in the service of a greater cause. The C.R.E. must come first—it's not something that's to be *used* for the private advantage of individuals, or even whole races. It's the most important thing that we humans have ever been involved in, and we have to be seen to be committed to it one hundred percent, or other races will *never* stop thinking of us as barbarians. Heaven knows, I'd *like* to help you, but I can't. Surely you can see that?"

"Listen, you stupid bastard," I said, in the most rational tone I could manage. "I'm going to get killed if I don't get out of this. *Killed.* D-E-A-D. I do not need lectures on the wonders of interracial cooperation. I need *help*."

"I'm sorry," he said—and he really did sound regretful. "I just can't do anything. Nothing that involves C.R.E., anyhow. Is there anything I can do without involving them?"

"No," I said tiredly. "Not a thing."

"I really am sorry," he said. "By the way, if it's any consolation, the war's over."

"What war?" I asked. My mind was on higher things.

"*The* war. My god, didn't you *know* we were at war?"

"Oh," I said. "That war. Who won?"

"Well," he said, "it's my considered opinion that no one won, or ever could win. The mere fact of having fought the war has done our standing in the galactic community irreparable harm. However, for what it's worth, we appear to have defeated the enemy. In fact, we appear to have wiped them out almost to the last man. We are now in possession of their homeworld."

"Great," I said. "That really makes me feel a lot better."

Actually, it didn't. It's a terrible thing to have to admit, but at that particular moment, I really didn't much care.

It wasn't until later that I realized how glad the news should have made me. After all, it was our winning the war that really saved my life.

It will not surprise you greatly to learn that there was no mad rush to buy me out. Under other circumstances, it would have been enough to make a man feel distinctly unloved, but things being what they were, I could take refuge in the theory that those who were genuinely concerned for my welfare were either too poor or too terrified to do anything about it.

While my period of grace ebbed slowly I tried desperately to think of a way out, but my imagination just wasn't up to it. It was all too neatly tied up. The only chance I had of short-term survival was selling myself to Amara Guur. I would have liked nothing better than to confound his evil plan (whatever it was) but I was damned if I was going to get myself killed or turned into a pharmaceuticals factory in order to do it.

I tried to console myself with the thought that at least I'd get to find out what the hell was going on, but it seemed a high price to pay for the satisfaction of a little innocent curiosity.

By the time the appointed hour rolled around (as appointed hours inevitably and inexorably do), I was feeling pretty fatalistic about the whole thing. Even the obvious attractions of the professional *femme fatale* Guur had sent to sugar the bitter pill failed to make my prospects seem any more alluring than they really were. I was taken out of my cell into the Hall of Justice itself, where the vital document was to be signed in the presence of an officiating magistrate, my not-so-trusty lawyer and my good friend 69-Aquila. They were all to witness that I was signing the contract of my own free will. (Hollow laughter is optional.)

While the magistrate was reading the document to me in

perfect *parole*, my eye was on the wall clock, watching the hundredths tick away. A Tetron standard day is about twenty-eight of our hours, and is divided up into a hundred units, each one of which is further subdivided by a further hundred. Each small unit, therefore, is approximately ten seconds long. Watching them tick over is like the legendary Chinese water torture.

They actually had the stylo and the fingerprint pad all ready for me when fate shook itself free from its downbeat rut and took one of those dramatic turns for which it is justly famous.

There was the sudden sound of ringing footsteps on the polished plastic floor, and into the hall swept half a dozen humans in neat black uniforms, headed by a blonde woman who gave the impression that she thought her wrathful stare ought to be turning everyone into stone.

"Russell!" she commanded. "Don't sign that paper!"

I wasn't about to quibble about the spelling of my name. I just stared at her. She came marching—*literally* marching—down the aisle, and her squad of starship troopers came marching after her. After them—trotting in order to keep up—came Aleksandr Sovorov.

Jacinthe Siani looked around, as if searching for moral support, but she was on her own. It wouldn't have mattered if she'd had a dozen of Guur's hatchet men with her. For one thing, it's a diplomatic gaffe to start riots in the Hall of Justice, in the presence of an officiating magistrate. For another, the star-captain and her six bravos were wearing flame pistols, and looked as if they knew how to use them.

The star-captain arrived at the foot of the platform, and vaulted up to join us by the table where our little ceremony was being conducted. She looked at Jacinthe Siani, curled her lip a little, and then looked away, radiating contempt. The Kythnan gritted her teeth.

"I'm Captain Susarma Lear of the Earth star-force," announced the blonde woman. "I want this man released into my custody. I'll pay what's necessary."

"You can't!" said Jacinthe Siani. "The deadline's expired. He has to sign the contract he's already accepted."

It didn't seem to me to be a time for legal niceties. I grabbed the offending document from the table, ripped it in half, and threw it at the Kythnan's feet. "I changed my mind before the deadline expired," I said. "I'll accept the star-captain's offer instead." I looked at the magistrate hopefully. The magistrate looked at 238-Zenatta.

238-Zenatta rose to the occasion. "I submit," he said, "that in the absence of any evidence to the contrary, we must accept Mr. Rousseau's submission that he did, in fact, alter his intentions before the expiry of the deadline. In any case, he had not affirmed that he was willing to sign the document, and cannot be held to have accepted Ms. Siani's contract formally."

"That seems to be a rational summation of the situation," agreed the magistrate. "If the star-captain can satisfy me that the conditions of the law will be upheld, I see no reason why she should not obtain the prisoner's release on her terms."

I looked Jacinthe Siani in the face, and beamed broadly. "It really breaks my heart to do it," I told her, "but I *love* women in uniform."

"You'll regret this," she hissed, her composure breaking a little under the strain.

"If I have anything to say about it," I assured her, "I'll be off this world before Amara Guur has a chance to start chewing the carpet."

The star-captain went into a huddle with 238-Zenatta and the magistrate. Meanwhile, Sovorov came up the steps to join me. The troopers stayed down below, watching Jacinthe Siani as she left the Hall, moving with a sense of urgency.

"Christ!" I said. "You don't half cut things fine. Where did you find her?"

"I didn't exactly *find* her," he replied. "She was thrust upon me. That officious idiot from Immigration Control called me and said that in view of the fact that Saul Lyndrach had disappeared and you were in jail, could I possibly sponsor a few short-term immigrants. I was about to refer them to someone else when the star-captain came on the line herself, and said that her business was too urgent to wait for bureaucratic niceties, and would I please get her through Control *immediately*. I thought I'd better do as she said."

"I can understand that," I muttered. "But how did you get her to buy me off?"

"Oh," he said, "it wasn't *my* idea." At this point the burst of unthinking admiration I'd been feeling disappeared like magic. "You see," he continued, "the first thing she asked me when I picked her up was where I could find Saul Lyndrach. I explained that he seemed to have disappeared. Then she explained that the person she was *really* looking for was the outworlder Lyndrach had taken in a few days ago. I explained that he was logged out through lock five during the early hours of last night, in your truck. Then. . . ."

"*He was what!*" I screeched. My heart was already pounding from the last shock I'd received. The thought that my truck had been hijacked drove clean out of my head the fact that I'd resolved to get off the planet without even bothering to change my clothes.

"I'm sorry," said Sovorov. "Didn't you know?"

"Of course I didn't know, you stupid bastard!"

"*I* didn't know you didn't know," he said, in an aggrieved tone.

"Never mind that," I said. "How did *you* know?"

"74-Scarion—the Immigration Control man—called me first thing . . . before the star-captain arrived, of course . . . to ask me if I knew whether Saul Lyndrach was aboard the truck with the outworlder. If he wasn't, you see, that would have been a technical breach of responsibility. Ordinarily, 74-Scarion wouldn't have bothered about it, but in view of the fact that there had already been some anxiety about the case. . . ."

"*Was* Saul with the outworlder?" I asked.

"How should I know?" he replied. "Anyway, I told the star-captain all this, and told her that you knew Lyndrach as well as anyone. I also told her that if she intended to go out in the cold chasing the outworlder, you were the best man to guide her. Also, I pointed out that you might want your truck back if you could be bought off the murder charge, and that would provide you and her with a kind of common cause."

By this time, things were moving a little too fast for my bewildered brain.

"How did he get the truck?" I asked. "The keys are in my room—the key to the truck, *and* to the lock-up."

Sovorov shrugged.

I didn't have time to pursue the mystery any further. The star-captain tapped me on the shoulder. "Okay," she said,

"You're out. The Tetrax are collecting their pound of flesh from my ship. Just remember that I'm not doing you any favors free, gratis and for nothing. You *owe* me. Sign these."

She presented me with a sheaf of papers—forms in triplicate, printed in English and Chinese.

I looked at them uncomprehendingly. "What are they?" I asked stupidly.

"They're your conscription papers," she said. "The star-force is about to make a man of you."

"I don't want . . ." I began. I gave up as the look in her bright blue eyes hardened into the kind of Gorgon stare she'd used to wither Jacinthe Siani.

I stared at the papers, wondering whether or not I was entitled to feel miserable.

"Didn't you tell me that your race had abandoned slavery several generations ago?" asked 69-Aquila, who was looking on with interest.

"Yeah," I said. "But I guess we're not such barbarians after all, are we?"

10

I didn't get a commission. I didn't even get a uniform. Star-captain Susarma Lear tucked my conscription papers away under her shirt, and led the way down the aisle, out into the glare of the dome's arc lights. Basic training lasted about half a minute, and consisted of her pointing to one of her merry men and saying: "That's Lieutenant Crucero. Anything he orders you to do, you *do*. I'm star-captain Lear. Anything *I* order you to do, you do. If you've any questions, forget 'em. Now, what do you know about the android?"

"What android?" I replied.

"The big one. The one that stole your truck. Seems to be going under the name of Myrlin."

"He's not human?" I queried.

"He's an android," she said. "That's two questions more than your ration. What do you know about him?"

"I've never even seen him," I told her. "I was asked to sponsor him for entry to the dome, but I passed him on to Saul Lyndrach. I tried to find Saul before I was fitted up for this lousy murder, but I couldn't. He'd dropped out of sight—so had the android until some stupid lock attendant let him out driving *my* truck. I only hope he tries to get into my cold-suit. That'll teach the bastard!"

"Why?" she inquired.

"Rumor has it," I said, "that he's half a meter taller than I am. Cold-suits don't stretch. Not *that* far, anyhow."

We paused outside the Hall.

"Where are we going?" she asked.

"Up the skychain to your ship," I replied hopefully. "Aren't we?"

"We came here after the android," she said. "We are going to get the android."

"He's out in the cold," I protested. "How the hell are you going to find him? We can't do anything until he comes back, and we'll be a damned sight more comfortable waiting aboard your ship than down here."

"Suppose he doesn't come back?" she said.

"Then you can stop worrying about him, can't you?"

She turned the flinty stare on me again.

"Look," I said, "I don't think you quite appreciate my situation. *Our* situation, that is. At this present moment, I am practically a walking target. So are you. You may not realize this, but I have enemies, and by snatching me from the jaws of disaster, you have made them into *your* enemies. It's not safe down here."

Her bleak eyes bored into the very nooks and crannies of my soul. "Trooper Russell," she said stonily, "you are in the starforce. Certainly, you have enemies. *We* have enemies. My ship has been on its present tour of duty for nineteen months, Earth-time, and we have spent that entire time facing enemies who had the resources of whole worlds to draw upon. We burned them. We burned whole worlds. The prospect of making enemies among the petty criminals of Skychain City does not worry us. Do you understand that?"

"*I* do," I assured her. "But Amara Guur might not."

"Where can I get in touch with the local law-enforcement

agencies?" she asked. That was a curious coincidence, because as she said it I was staring over her shoulder at the approaching road strip, which was at that very moment bearing toward us three representatives of the law: Tetron peace officers, sporting mindscramblers. Ordinarily, that would not be a sight to strike terror into the heart of an innocent citizen such as myself, but from the moment they had come into sight their eyes had been fixed on me.

When I didn't answer her question, the star-captain looked over her shoulder. She looked pleased, but the peace officers ignored her as they leapt nimbly from the strip, and their spokesman addressed himself to me.

"Are you Mr. Michael Rousseau?" he asked.

"I didn't do it," I said.

"You are not under suspicion of having committed any crime at the present time," he informed me dutifully. "However, we are investigating a multiple murder, and the fact that your name has been linked with those of several of the victims necessitates our asking you some routine questions. It will not be necessary for you to accompany us to our offices, provided that you have no objection to our recording your answers here."

The star-captain was giving me a rather peculiar look, as if she were wondering whether she'd accidentally conscripted Jack the Ripper.

"Who's dead this time?" I asked.

"Seven men appear to have been killed in all," the policeman told me. "Three are vormyr, one is a Spirellan, one a human, and two are Zabarans. Three of the persons gave evidence recently at a trial—your trial. All three testified that they were present when you battered to death a Sleath following an argument about a card game."

"Balidar's dead?" I said weakly. It was certainly a big day for surprises.

"Simeon Balidar is the deceased human," confirmed the peace officer. "The Spirellan named Lema also testified against you, as did a Zabaran named Shian Mor."

My first thought, I have to admit, was slight disappointment that Heleb apparently wasn't numbered among the dead.

"You know it wasn't me," I told him. "I was in jail. Ask Aquila whatever-his-number-is."

"I have said that you are not under suspicion," replied the Tetron, frowning about the discourteous way I'd referred to his species-cousin. "All I wish to ask you is whether you know anything about the crime. Do you know of anyone other than yourself who might have anything against these men?"

"I know nothing whatsoever about the crime," I said truthfully. "The dead men were participants in a conspiracy to pervert the course of justice by having me convicted of a crime I did not commit. I believe that the conspiracy was headed by Amara Guur. Perhaps you should ask him who might have wanted to see his agents dead. Or is he one of the dead vormyr?"

The peace officer didn't seem too happy about the statement I had made, but he recorded it all dutifully.

"Amara Guur is not among the deceased," he said, politely answering my question. "Do you have any evidence of the truth of what you say?"

"Certainly," I replied. "I can say with absolute confidence that I did not murder the Sleath, and that I was framed. I have the evidence of my own memory and my own senses. I need no other."

The star-captain obviously thought that her time was being wasted.

"Are you intending to charge this man?" she demanded.

"No," replied the peace officer.

"In that case, you have no right to question him without my permission. This man is a trooper in the Earth star-force, and I am his superior officer. As it happens, though, I want some information which you can probably provide. I want to know the whereabouts of a stolen vehicle. I also want your cooperation in apprehending and extraditing the thief."

"I fear," said the officer, "that I am at present engaged in conducting a murder inquiry, and am consequently unable to assist you. If you care to call our offices from any convenient wall phone, I'm sure someone will be available to discuss this matter with you. Am I to understand that I may not question this man further at the present time?"

"Yes, you are," she snapped back. "We have our own business to attend to."

"This is duly noted," said the Tetron, in a tone that was only faintly aggrieved. "I may get in touch with you again."

He turned away and hopped back onto the strip, which carried him away in the company of his two fellow officers.

Star-captain Lear looked back at me.

"If you were to ask me," I said amicably, "I'd suggest that we do a little investigating of our own. To get the keys to the truck, he would have had to break into my room. I'd like to get back there and see what else he stole. Maybe there's something there that will help us. Also, I'm hungry. Back there, we can get something to eat."

"I thought you were scared to travel the streets in case of attempted assassination?" she said, a fraction derisively.

"I am," I assured her. "But you're not going to let me go up to your ship, are you? Besides which, it seems that we're not the only ones on the side of the angels. Someone has started assassinating the would-be assassins. I don't know who it is, but I wish him every success in his future endeavors. Do we go to my place?"

"We do," she said grimly. I got the impression that she didn't altogether approve of me, but wasn't about to say so—yet.

It took twenty minutes to get home, and the time passed without assassination attempts. I led the captain and her troopers into my room—which showed no sign of having been broken into—and was just about to relax into the secure feeling that you get from familiar surroundings when I noticed something distinctly unfamiliar about them.

There was somebody in my bed.

It was Saul Lyndrach, and he looked extremely dead.

11

I will not bore you with a full account of every word that was exchanged before evening in pursuit of an explanation for the presence of Saul Lyndrach (deceased) in my bed. Let it suffice to say that the Tetrax conducted their investigation with commendable thoroughness, and reached the following series of conclusions.

Item One. Lyndrach had died at approximately twelve eighty that morning, while I was still asleep in my cell. This was approximately two hours after Myrlin had left lock five in my truck—seven units in Tetron time. According to the Tetron pathologist, however, he would have been unconscious for several hours before his death.

Item Two. The reason Saul Lyndrach would have been unconscious for several hours before he died was that he was a very sick man. The reason that he was very sick was that he had (apparently) been subjected to torture. According to the pathologist, the torture had begun some days before—not long after Saul had agreed to take in the homeless android.

Item Three. *Before* lapsing into unconsciousness, Lyndrach had used my phone to make a series of important purchases. He had bought an outsize cold-suit, and supplies enough to stock my truck for a journey lasting several hundred days (Tetron time). In fact, he had used up virtually all the credit he had in so doing. The goods had been delivered to the lock-up where my truck was kept.

Item Four. Neither Saul Lyndrach nor the individual calling himself Myrlin had requested medical assistance. Saul had, however, left a message addressed to me on the display screen by my phone. It read: Dear Mike, We have no idea where you are, and can't ask your permission, but we need your truck badly. We can't get to mine, but after we're gone, you'll be able to. It's yours. I think the exchange is fair, sorry if it turns out otherwise. Saul. (We inferred from this that Saul was unaware of my arrest, and that he expected to be taking the trip along with Myrlin. But why, we asked ourselves, couldn't Saul get to his own truck?)

That was just about all, except for one initially unrelated fact that one of the peace officers happened to let drop in the course of the conversation. Simeon Balidar and the other six dead men whose murders were connected with his had been smashed up like rag dolls. No one had used a weapon against them. Whoever had done it must have been immensely strong, even if he'd taken them one at a time.

By the time I'd added all that up, I had a pretty good idea

who had done what and when, but I still had no idea why. Even at that, I seemed to be one step ahead of the peace officers, though you can never tell with the Tetrax.

My room was still very crowded after the Tetrax had gone, taking Saul Lyndrach's body with them. It wasn't a very big room, and it hadn't been designed for large-scale dinner parties. The star-captain and her troopers didn't seem to mind, and they didn't bother to ask whether I minded or not. We ate sitting on the floor—the star-force, thankfully, paid for the food.

"How long will it be before they apprehend the android?" asked star-captain Lear.

"What makes you think they're going to chase him?" I asked.

She looked startled, and I realized that she really didn't know much about the way things worked on Asgard. "He's a murderer!" she said.

"He's disappeared into the darkside of a very large planet," I said. "He not only has the run of the surface, but the lower levels too. The Tetrax wouldn't stand a cat in hell's chance of catching up with him. Why should they bother? If he ever comes back, they'll question him about the events of the last few days, but in the meantime it's a simple matter of out of sight, out of mind."

"For Christ's sake!" she said. "He'll hardly take much finding. They must be able to track him from the docking satellite."

"Not on the darkside," I said. "Anyhow, as I said—why would they bother? He's innocent until proven guilty. The Tetrax have no proof that he's murdered anyone, and even if they knew for sure they'd hardly commit the kind of force that would be required to the job of catching him."

The star-captain didn't reply. I could tell that she was thinking.

"As a matter of interest," I said. "Who do you think he murdered?"

"Saul Lyndrach, of course," she replied.

"You've got it all wrong," I told her. "He murdered everyone *except* Saul. Balidar, Lema and that crowd. He murdered *them* when he sprang Saul, sometime yesterday. If you can call it murder—I call it heroism. Definitely self-defense. Amara Guur murdered Saul. Not personally, of course, but it was his doing. It must have been."

She looked at me through narrowed eyes. "How do you know?" she asked.

"Logical deduction," I told her. "Quite elementary, really. All you need is the initial premise—which one can more or less take for granted around here—that whenever anything nasty happens, the vormyr are behind it. Guur's men must have snatched Saul not long after he took Myrlin off 74-Scarion's hands. They can hardly have expected to find Myrlin, but they either took him along for the ride or dumped him somewhere. They probably shot Saul and him with anaesthetic darts to avoid the possibility of objections. The only trouble was, Myrlin was a lot tougher to handle than they figured. One way or another, he got his chance to fight back. He got Saul free, but Saul must have been in pretty bad shape. With Guur's trigger-men out they couldn't go back to his place, and they didn't dare go to the lock-up where his truck was. Instead, they went looking for help, and came here—not knowing that Guur was fitting me up too. Saul would have known how to get past the lock—he was clever with his hands. Then he began to set things up for his getaway, using my truck. Only he couldn't make it. He must have conked out, leaving Myrlin wondering what to do. He should have called a doctor—or somebody—but maybe he just didn't know how. At the very worst, he simply let Saul die without making an effort to save him. He didn't kill him."

"I think," said Susarma Lear slowly, "that you'd better explain to me exactly what is going on around here."

"What I'd like," I countered, "is an explanation of what exactly you're doing here."

She did her Medusa impression again. "Trooper," she said, in a taut voice, "in the star-force, you don't talk that way to an officer. I ask the questions."

I decided to be generous and forgive her. After all, it was only a few hours since she'd saved my life.

"Okay," I said, being sweetly reasonable. "I'll tell you anything I can. Unfortunately, I don't think I can add much to what I've already said. I presume that Guur snatched Saul because Saul found something big when he was out in the cold.

There have been rumors flying around Alex Sovorov's academy of sages. At a guess, Saul found a way down to levels lower than we've previously managed to reach. Maybe he found a way to go a *long* way down. That's what we all spend our lives looking for, and I'd say that Saul was a better bet than most to come up with the goods. The one thing I still can't figure at all is why Guur wanted me too. Obviously I know something I don't know I know, if you get my meaning. That's just about all I can tell you."

"What are these levels you keep talking about?" she asked.

I was stunned. It just hadn't occurred to me that she didn't know the first thing about Asgard. I had assumed, without really thinking about it, that everybody in the universe knew about Asgard.

"The surface of this world is an artificial construction," I told her. "It's one of a series of shells. Nobody knows, but it's possible the whole world is artificial, and that it's built up entirely of shells. The next level down—level one—has five major networks of caves, each one the size of a continent. There are several known points where we can descend to level two, and it's not too difficult to penetrate three and four. The only problem is that they're very cold. People lived there once, but they went away. Most people think they went lower down, sheltering from the catastrophe that destroyed the outer atmosphere and froze the upper levels. That must have happened a long, long time ago—maybe millions of years, maybe hundreds of millions—but some people would like to believe that they're still down there somewhere, in the center. We make our living here scavenging among the things they left behind them, which have been preserved by the cold in pretty good condition. To us, it's new technology. Institutes like the C.R.E.—coordinated research establishment—are trying to build a coherent picture of what the culture was like, and the knowledge that lay behind its technology. That's what we're all here for."

"I see," she said. She didn't. She couldn't see anything but the tiniest fraction of what it was all about. I could see that I was going to have to do a lot of explaining. She continued: "You've been out on the surface many times, I take it. Exploring these lower levels."

"Yes I have," I told her.

"That's good," she said. "You'll be able to advise us when we go after the android."

I'd known all along that she was going to say that. It had a kind of inevitability about it. I should have been absolutely aghast, but instead I simply shook my head.

"It can't be done," I said. "We stand no better chance of tracking him down than the Tetrax."

"We have to do it," she said.

"Why?" I asked.

"I can't tell you that. But that android must be found."

"What would you do if you found him?"

"Kill him," she said flatly.

"I've got nothing against him," I said. "Not a damn thing."

"You're a trooper in the star-force," she reminded me yet again. "That's reason enough. That android must be destroyed."

"It doesn't matter how hard you snarl," I told her. "Impossible is impossible. There's no way we can figure out where he's gone. No way at all."

There was a moment's silence. Then she said: "Trooper Russell, I have every reason to think that the star-force—if it is necessary in order to destroy that android—would be prepared to bomb this world out of existence."

I looked at her, wondering whether or not she was completely insane. In the end, all I could think of to say was: "My name is Rousseau, not Russell. It was French, originally."

"Do you realize now the magnitude of the problem?" she inquired solemnly.

"Sure," I said. "Having exterminated one humanoid species, you're now willing to take on three hundred more, including the Tetrax. We'd only be outnumbered by—at a conservative estimate—several millions to one. And that's people. In terms of worlds, ships and weaponry we'd be outclassed right out of sight. Lady, if you so much as take the safety catch off your flame pistol on this world, you're in danger of creating a diplomatic incident. If you repeat what you just said to anyone, especially a Tetron, you're likely to find yourself back aboard your ship heading for nowhere with instructions never to cast a backward glance in this direction. Who the hell do you think you are?"

The silence that descended then seemed very heavy. I could almost swear that the troopers stopped breathing. They seemed positively spellbound. I thought the star-captain might be about to go berserk, but it turned out that she wasn't *that* mad.

"My orders," she said, civilly enough, "are to do everything in my power to apprehend and destroy that android. *Everything.*"

"In that case," I pointed out, "you'd better do some very precise figuring about exactly where your power stops—because it stops a damn sight shorter than you think it does. Are you from Earth?"

"Yes I am," she said.

"Have you ever been on an alien world before?"

"Several. But I think I get the drift of your argument. No, Trooper *Rousseau,* I'm not experienced in dealing with other humanoid races, except for the enemy we have just defeated. I do not intend to conduct myself here with any undue recklessness. My statement about the lengths to which star-force might be prepared to go was simply intended to impress upon you the importance of my mission. That android actually poses a threat to the future of the entire human race."

"I think we outnumber him by several millions to one," I said. "Even if he *is* strong enough to smash Guur's hatchet men seven at a time. How superhuman can he be? I take it he was put together by our defeated foes?"

"That's correct," she said.

"Well," I said, "logic would tend to suggest that he can't be all *that* dangerous, or we wouldn't have won the war, would we?"

"The fact remains," she said stubbornly, "that my orders are to kill him at all costs. And *you* are going to do everything in *your* power to make sure I do. Is that clear?"

There are some people you just can't argue with. Not all of them are Tetrax.

I was about to go on to explain that even I, wonderful though I am on my better days, couldn't do the impossible, when the phone buzzed. I got up to answer it, and when I lifted the receiver the call came through on visual as well as audio. The image on the screen was that of a vormyr.

All vormyr look pretty much alike to the untutored human

eye, but I wouldn't have needed three guesses to tell who this one was.

"Mr. Rousseau?" he inquired, in badly-broken *parole*. "My name is Amara Guur."

12

Politeness required that I should switch on the eye above my own phone, so that he could see me too. I didn't bother. I felt that I could quite happily live out my life without ever standing face-to-face with Amara Guur.

"What do you want?" I asked harshly.

He smiled. The vormyr are a predatory species, irredeemably carnivorous. I'm told they have extremely bad breath. Anyhow, they have the kind of teeth that go with their diet. Guur looked like a cross between a wolf and a crocodile—it wasn't a particularly harmonious combination. His smile wasn't at all attractive.

"I have a gift for you," he said.

"Keep it," I replied.

"I couldn't do that," he said. "It's rightfully your property— if, as I understand, you're the beneficiary of Saul Lyndrach's will."

"What the hell are you talking about?" I asked. The expression lost a little in translation, but he seemed to get the drift.

"It's a little something he . . . left in my charge." So saying, he lifted something up to the eye, so that I could see it. It was a black notebook. Saul's log. It must contain the record of his last trip, I figured. It had to be a genuine, twenty-four carat treasure map. But why, I wondered, was Amara Guur volunteering to hand it over to me?

"I don't understand," I said.

"You will," he promised.

"If you think that's bait enough to get me to walk into a trap," I told him, "you're very much mistaken."

"I don't," he said. "It will be handed over to you, if you want it, in a public place, in the full glare of daylight. You may bring along your protective escort, flame pistols and all. I will send Jacinthe, quite unarmed. You will forgive me if I do not come myself. I should not like to be linked with Saul Lyndrach, in view of his unfortunate accidental death. It *was* accidental, I assure you."

"Just like the Sleath," I said.

He smiled again. "I apologize most sincerely for any inconvenience I may inadvertently have caused you," he said. "However, I know nothing whatsoever about any Sleath. Incidentally, it would not be to your advantage to inform the peace officers regarding any arrangement we might make. If they obtain possession of the book you never will. The Tetrax are irredeemably honest, but they have an eye to their own advantage which rarely fails them. If you want to know what Saul Lyndrach knew, then be in the plaza to the west of the skychain at fifty-zero-zero tomorrow."

"Like hell I will," I told him, hoping he'd pick up the negative connotations of the phrase.

"Think it over, Mr. Rousseau," he said. Then he switched off.

I put the receiver back in its nest, slowly. As the star-captain opened her mouth, I raised my hand. "Don't ask me to explain," I said. "I haven't a clue. All I know is that Amara Guur never gives anything away, unless it's lethal. No power in the universe is going to make me turn up for that appointment."

"You don't have to go," said Susarma Lear. "I'll go instead."

"Why?" I asked.

"Because," she said, "that book may tell us where the android has gone."

"It might," I agreed. "But if it does, why would Guur simply hand it over to us?"

"I don't know," she answered. "But if what you say is true, it's the only chance of finding him that we have. I have to take that chance."

"Have it your own way," I said with a shrug. "You're welcome."

"You're coming with me," she said.

"You just said I didn't have to!" I protested.

"I've decided that I want you where I can see you. It occurs to me that if I leave you here, you might somehow get lost. I think we'll stay together, at least until we have more reason to trust one another. We'll all go to this plaza tomorrow, but I'll collect the book. I don't think Guur is going to try to kill you. The simple fact that he appeared on that screen, and talked to you, knowing that witnesses could hear what he was saying, seems to indicate that he's playing a more complicated game. If you did get killed, after his making that call, he could hardly avoid being accused of the crime, even if he avoided conviction. Doesn't *your* reasoning assure you of that?"

I had to admit—if only to myself—that she had a point. Guur, for whatever reason, had abandoned his usual policies and deliberately come out into the open. Even from him, that was some kind of guarantee of good faith. But what could he possibly hope to gain? I was extremely curious, and it didn't do me a bit of good to know that Guur had done his level best to *make* me curious.

"The hell with it," I said. "I'm in this too deep. I'll put my stupid head on the block, right alongside yours. What can *I* possibly have against living dangerously?"

"Now," she said, "you're starting to talk like a member of the star-force."

I couldn't help remembering the wise words of my good friend 69-Aquila. It's when they start to agree with you that you begin to worry.

13

Mercifully, I managed to get the use of another room in the same section of the stack, so that at least there weren't eight of us trying to sleep in mine. Star-captain Lear insisted on posting a guard in the corridor, though I wasn't altogether clear in my own mind whether he was there to stop assassins from getting in, to stop me from getting out, or to provide a good excuse for only having three people sharing my room. The star-captain also commandeered my bed, leaving Lieutenant Crucero and myself to share the floor. Rank has its privileges.

The next morning, the star-captain began making arrangements for an expedition into the cold. The keys to Saul Lyndrach's truck were in the drawer from which mine had been taken—a fair exchange, as he'd promised. I explained to the captain, however, that under no circumstances was one truck going to carry more than three people. I persuaded her that one more would probably suffice, though she'd have to abandon two of her bully boys in Skychain City. When I gave her the list of equipment we were going to need, she looked it over suspiciously, but once you've undertaken to pay for a truck, why balk at six cold-suits, with a full stock of supplies and a set of the tools of the trade (my trade, that is)? When the Tetrax accepted her promissory notes on behalf of star-force, I had mixed feelings. On the one hand, I wasn't really looking forward to chasing wild geese in her company, but on the other hand, if everything went in my favor, I might end the day with all my equipment problems solved. (I was assuming, of course, that I could get around little problems like my having been conscripted into the star-force. Myrlin wasn't the only one who could disappear into the wilderness when the appropriate moment arrived.)

Shortly before midday, we went uptown to the plaza in front of the skychain dock. The star-captain left Crucero in charge of the supply problem, and took two of her troopers to stand guard over us in the event of trouble. One was an oriental named Khalekhan, the other a character of uncertain ancestry named Serne. They were, I gathered, ground-fighters who'd seen a good deal of action. They probably weren't good at anything else, but killing people was a skill they'd cultivated fairly carefully. Despite these qualifications, they didn't make me feel secure. Amara Guur was far too subtle to try anything within *their* area of expertise.

The wait was thoroughly boring. One bit of Skychain City looks exactly like another, and the fact that the plaza was the largest open space under the dome didn't really make it a tourist attraction. The Skychain itself, of course, was above the dome, and all we could see from the plaza was the stack that supported the baseplate. The only thing that happened to relieve the tedium was a roadstrip accident caused by a Campanulan attempting a double switch. He lost his balance, brought down three others of assorted races, and dropped something into the roller-gears that jammed up the works and brought enough safety-relays into operation to stop the arterial strips for half a kilometer in every direction.

"Great," I commented. "Now we're going to have to walk to the next intersection before we can ride home."

"Does that happen often?" asked Susarma Lear, her steely gaze wandering over the entire scene, measuring the carnage.

"About twice a day," I told her. "The repair crews have got it down to a fine art now. They'll have everything working again in an hour. It only takes longer if some stupid idiot gets an arm or a leg trapped."

Jacinthe Siani was a little late—presumably because of the traffic snarl-up. I didn't see her until she was almost on top of us because of the crowd that was forming on the pedwalk. When the strips stop, the pedwalk fills up pretty quickly, especially in a place like the plaza.

The star-captain rested her right hand lightly on her firearm as the Kythnan woman approached, but Jacinthe Siani's eyes were fixed on me.

She came right up to me, and produced the black notebook from the pocket of her jacket.

"There you are, Mr. Rousseau," she said. "It's all yours. As far as we can tell, you're the only man in Skychain City who can use it. You're a very lucky man."

I took the notebook rather gingerly, as if I half-expected it to bite. She made no attempt to move away yet, but simply stood waiting, her hands by her sides.

I opened the book at random, and let the pages flutter through my fingers. Enlightenment struck me like a blow on the head as the last piece of the puzzle fell into place. Saul Lyndrach had kept his log in French. Out of the three hundred or so humans living in Skychain City, there would be plenty who knew English, Russian, Japanese or Chinese. But take three hundred individuals at random out of the population of Earth and all her colonies, and how many are likely to know French?

In this particular case, the answer was two. That was the expertise that Amara Guur had tried to obtain. He had tortured Saul to make him tell, but Saul hadn't cracked. Not only hadn't he cracked, but in so doing he'd persuaded Guur that it would pay him to try less direct methods with me.

I looked up at Jacinthe Siani. She was watching me, with a half-smile on her exquisite face.

"Why?" I said. "Why hand it over?"

"It's not so secret anymore," she said. "If we had time, we could find a way of getting the information, but we haven't. We didn't anticipate the giant's involvement. Lyndrach must have told him everything. Before long, the route to the center will be as busy as an arterial road strip. This is no use to us any longer—we thought you might like it, as a gesture of good will. An apology, if you like."

"Oh sure," I said. "The real plan is that you expect me to go chasing after Myrlin before nightfall. You lost your chance to track him, but with sufficient forewarning you think highly of your chances of tracking *us*. We catch Myrlin, you catch us, and firepower wins the big prize. Some apology."

"Have it your own way," she said, with a full smile. She stepped back, but she wasn't looking where she was going, and a Noemian in a hurry barged straight into her, practically knocking her off her feet. She staggered right into the star-captain, who caught her and stood her upright again. For once, their expressions matched as they both seemed startled. The star-captain had acted reflexively, and now she shoved the Kythnan away, almost as though she were resisting some kind of pollution. They exchanged another matched glance of incipient hatred. Then Jacinthe Siani hurried away, and was lost in the crowd.

I looked at the star-captain, wondering if she understood what had just happened, and whether I ought to tell her if she didn't. I decided that the answer to both questions was probably negative.

There was probably a microtransmitter in the book, and by now there was at least one more planted on the star-captain. That was okay by me. There were a dozen ways that Guur could track us over the surface, if he desperately wanted to. Down below, it would be a different matter. If there really was a route down into the center, there would probably be a hundred opportunities to abandon both the book *and* the star-captain. Out there, I would be in my element—and whatever

Amara Guur or Susarma Lear might think, the advantages would lie with me.

"Okay," I said to the star-captain. "This will probably tell us where the android went. We can start just as soon as you want to."

14

We logged out of lock five a few minutes before the Tetrax were scheduled to switch off the city's "daylight" and go over to the reduced lighting of "night." Outside, it was still twelve hours until dawn.

We headed north across the vast level plain that surrounds the city on all sides. Serne and the star-captain were riding with me. Crucero, Khalekhan and a man named Vasari were following in the second vehicle. We were in communication with the other truck, and with Susarma Lear's warship, which was linked to the satellite complex at the top of the skychain. The chain itself was invisible in the black night.

The lights of the truck played over a featureless carpet of white, which lay almost dead flat. There were no shadows at all.

"God!" said Susarma Lear, after we'd been traveling for an hour. "Is it all like this?"

"Pretty much," I said. "We need the direction-finder to operate with a high degree of precision. It's not easy taking bearings in the middle of Asgard night when the sky's blank. There aren't any landmarks, and the snow covers just about everything. It isn't as flat as it looks, of course. There are no mountains or valleys, but there are shallow troughs and hollows. You'll see that at midday, when the snow's all melted."

She was sitting beside me, staring up through the canopy at the sky.

"Is it really as black and starless as that?" she asked. "Or is it just cloud?"

"It's starless," I told her. "We're right on the edge of the galactic arm here, and at this time of year the night sky is almost completely dark. There are a few stars that show close to the horizon, but overhead there's nothing but infinite darkness. It's not empty, mind—just dark. With a telescope, you can pick up a few other galaxies. Not the black one, though—that needs an X-ray 'scope."

"What black one?" she asked.

I looked sideways at her. "You really don't know a goddamn thing about this world, do you?" I said.

"How could I?" she replied sharply.

"You really never heard of the black galaxy?"

"Vaguely," she answered, defensively.

"It's the modest member of our little galactic family," I told her. "It's about a hundred and twenty thousand light-years away, closer than the Magellanic clouds but not so obvious. It's getting even closer—heading toward us at something like thirty thousand meters per second. It'll take a hundred million years and more to get here, though, so there's not much cause for us to worry about it. It's basically just a heterogeneous cloud of dust, like the clouds inside our own galaxy, but more so. It has a very low temperature overall, though that varies a lot—there are a few stars inside it, but their light all gets soaked up before it reaches us. It's famous, in its own small way. Our galaxy's dark companion—the shadow galaxy that will one day engulf the greater part of our spiral arm. That's not to say, of course, that Earth—or any other world—will necessarily suffer the same kind of catastrophe that overwhelmed Asgard in the dim and distant past."

"What kind of catastrophe?" she inquired.

I sighed. "As you may have noticed by glancing at the pressure gauge," I said, "we are not rolling through a vacuum. In fact, when the heat of day has dispelled the snow, you will see that the surface of Asgard is not entirely lifeless. Once upon a time—even Aleksandr Sovorov doesn't claim to know how long ago—there was abundant life on the surface. Life as we know it, in fact, operating by the familiar processes of photosynthesis. The atmosphere was not unlike what we and most of the other humanoid species we can actually talk to are used to. There was plenty of oxygen.

"Then, by an accident of cosmic happenstance—or so we presume—Asgard ran into a cold cloud, composed mostly of hydrogen with a seasoning of cosmic debris. Cometary ices and the like. You can imagine what happened. Over a period of time, more and more hydrogen got added to the atmosphere, which got steadily colder. Asgard's sun probably began behaving strangely, but that may not have bothered the people much, owing to the fact that the intervention of the cloud would have made its influence much less noticeable. The surface may have warmed up a bit when the atmosphere caught fire, but that would have been a rather fleeting glow. All the oxygen in the atmosphere was soaked up by the cloud gases, to fall as the gentle rain from heaven. In time, it seems, the atmosphere itself began to condense. For a long period, the nitrogen and the ammonia and the other trace gases were themselves solidified, blowing over the desert surface as snow.

"Despite what people say about the beneficial effects of being deep-frozen, the planet's life system reacted quite badly to this chain of events. When the great freeze was finally over, there was little of it left to begin the job of reclaiming the surface. I suppose we might be grateful that there was anything at all. With a little help from the Tetrax, the plants are flourishing now—they've adapted very well to being frozen every night —and they're slowly working away at the problem of making the atmosphere breathable again. Much of the hydrogen has already drifted away into space, and the methane levels are really quite tolerable. In a few thousand years—less if the Tetrax are successful in their endeavors—it will be possible once again for humanoids to romp around on the surface of Asgard. In the daytime, anyway."

"And it was to escape this catastrophe that the natives dug themselves into the heart of the planet?"

"Well now," I said, "there you touch on the subject matter of several controversies. Everything I've said so far is what we *know*. There are, however, some rather odd things that we *don't* know. Opinions vary. For one thing, we're not entirely sure where Asgard was when all of this went on."

I don't think she was actually capable of looking innocently astonished. Whenever I said something that surprised her she looked at me as if I'd perpetrated an act of aggression—as if telling her something new and strange was a subtle kind of malevolence aimed at upsetting her balanced view of the universe.

"You mean it wasn't here?" she asked, as though the notion was slightly disgusting.

"I didn't say that. Some people believe that it *was* here, and has always been here, contentedly circling its present sun. The one problem with that contention is the mystery of the vanishing dust cloud. It clearly isn't here, nor is it in the immediate interstellar neighborhood. So—if you believe that Asgard is now where it has always been, you have to invent a secondary hypothesis to account for the missing cloud. Any such hypothesis hinges on the problem of how long it has been since the catastrophe, and no one knows that. There *are* dust clouds within a few hundred light-years away, but there isn't one which is moving away from this star in a way that suggests that it once might have passed through the system. One or two of them *might* be fitted up for the job, if something funny has happened to them in the last few million years—but that requires another secondary hypothesis. So maybe—just maybe—Asgard was somewhere else when it suffered its catastrophe."

"Where?" she wanted to know.

I pointed straight up.

"The black galaxy?"

"That's one of the favorites. Once you assume that the planet's moved, you might as well assume that it's come from somewhere interesting."

"But you said the black galaxy is moving *toward* us."

"And so it is. The hypothesis requires that the planet come on ahead. The idea is that Asgard originally circled a star in a clear area of the black galaxy—a star on this edge, from which it was possible to see the Milky Way. Its inhabitants, so the argument goes, realized that they were about to be engulfed by cloud, and that the engulfment might last more or less forever. In the short term, it's argued, they couldn't do much about it. So they made long-term plans to accelerate their world out of its own galaxy, toward ours. In the meantime, in order to be around when they reached their destination, they retired to the center, probably putting themselves into suspended animation."

"That's crazy!"

"Maybe so," I agreed. "But it's really not that much less likely than the hocus-pocus that's needed to solve the mystery of the missing dust cloud."

"How are they supposed to have moved the world? With rockets?"

"No. By some application of the frame force. Effectively, by using some variant of the wormhole drive."

"You can't put something the size of a planet into a wormhole," she said confidently.

"There's no theoretical limit to the mass you can wormhole," I told her. "It's just that it gets very energy-expensive to do. We don't find it economical to make starships any bigger than the ships that used to sail our oceans back home, but some races do. Generally, it's cheaper to build a hundred ships of ten tons each than it is to build one ship of a thousand tons, and collectively the little ships use far less energy than the big one. But if you have energy to spare, you might not care about balancing the budget."

"It's ridiculous!" she said. "You'd need the power of a star to put a whole planet into a wormhole."

"You'd need a *small* star," I agreed. "And a plentiful supply of hydrogen to feed it. But then, even we poor humans have a few small stars under our control. They're *very* small, I admit, but we do have them. Some of the other races we know have made artificial suns, of a sort."

"What you're trying to tell me," she said, in an aggrieved tone—presumably because I wasn't putting it baldly enough—"is that there's a gigantic fusion reactor somewhere inside this planet?"

"That's right," I agreed.

"I suppose they hollowed out their world in order to make a chamber for it? Or was it hollow already?"

"That," I said, "is another bone of contention. You see, the people who go in for this moving-planet type of hypothesis aren't the kind to boggle at a few more big ideas. The conservatives, of course, reckon that, at heart, Asgard is a perfectly normal planet, and that there are only a limited number of artificial levels built on top of the original surface. Those at the opposite extreme reckon that the whole thing is an artifact, from top to bottom, as it were. They think the levels go all the way down. In their view, Asgard is a kind of do-it-yourself Dyson sphere. Instead of building a vast shell round an already existing sun, they contend, Asgard's builders made a much more convenient size of shell, and then lit a sun inside it. You lose less space that way."

"Wouldn't it be rather hot in the lowest levels?" she asked.

"Hot as hell," I agreed. "Vast amounts of energy generated. But then—that's exactly what they'd need, wouldn't they, if the whole thing was going to wormhole its way around the galactic cluster. As you've already pointed out, it takes a lot of energy to warp enough space to slip a planet into the subspatial matrix."

She shook her head in embittered wonderment. "Does all that really make sense?" she asked, her tone suggesting that it had no right to make any sense at all.

"Some say that it does," I assured her. "I claim to be an agnostic, myself. After all, there's no proof one way or the other—yet. But in my heart, I can't help cherishing the fond hope that even the wildest stories err on the conservative side. I'd like to know the truth, whatever it is, but some kinds of truth are so much more exciting than others."

"In order to do all that," said the star-captain, "they'd have to have a technology way ahead of ours. But I suppose they do —otherwise there wouldn't be so many people here digging it up."

"Actually," I said, "they wouldn't need to be that far ahead. That is, they really wouldn't have to *know* a great deal more. They'd just have to be clever in applying it. And they were clever all right. We aren't grubbing around here looking for devices that work miracles—just for things that do the things we want to do a little better than the things we have for doing them. People tend to think of technology as something that's generated rather passively from knowledge, but it's not. Important inventions that can change the world in their manifold applications quite often emerge from knowledge that's been around for a long time. The Greeks could have built steam engines, if they had wanted to or needed to. The electric battery was probably invented first in the Classical Age, but it was lost again because the need wasn't strong enough. If you were to visit the homeworlds of any ten of the humanoid races gathered here, you'd almost certainly find that they had very different patterns of technological development, though they'd all possess much the same knowledge about the way the universe works. We think of technology as applied *science*, but that word 'applied' tends to conceal the fact that technology is first and foremost an *art*. There are a million ways to design every simple thing, like a fastener, or a switch, or a door. People get so hypnotized by the familiar ways of doing things that they become blinded to the fact that there might be dozens of other ways of achieving the same ends, some of them better. The history of technology isn't at all like the history of scientific *theory*, when you come to look at it—it's much more like the history of painting. Schools of architecture, for instance, aren't only schools of art, based on aesthetic considerations, they're schools of technology, different ways of connecting ends and means.

"We're not here on Asgard because the men of Asgard *knew* so very much more than we did. We're here because they were consummate artists, and because their technology can tell us a great deal about the very various ways we might apply the knowledge we already have.

"If we *did* find out, of course, that the men who built the levels had knowledge that we don't have, that would be something else. That would be a whole new ball game. But it's not necessary for that to be the case before we can justify our interest in the stuff we haul out of the levels. Nor is it necessary to assume they had any more knowledge than we have in order to credit them with the ability to make an artificial world—even one *this* big—and warp it into an intergalactic wormhole. The big problem with *that* hypothesis is rather more basic. You see, if all that is true, Asgard has now reached its destination. It has at least a breathing space of a hundred million years before the cloud catches up with it. So where, if this story is true, have they got to? Why don't they come out of hiding? If they *did* put themselves into suspended animation, *why haven't they woken up?*"

She was silent for a few moments, absorbing the details of the fantastic tale. I could see that in spite of her reflexive hostile reaction she was really quite captivated by the magic of it. Everybody is. I suppose, in the final analysis, *that's* why we're all here.

She turned her big blue eyes on me, and for once she didn't look like a snake trying to hypnotize a mouse.

"Perhaps," she said, "their private sun went out. Perhaps it isn't just the top levels that were frozen by the cloud. Perhaps the cold goes as deep as it's possible to go."

"Until today," I told her, "I always thought that was a possibility. I never wanted to believe it, but I had to consider it. But now I know it's not true."

"How?" she asked, though she would have been able to guess if she could have spared a moment's thought.

I tapped Saul Lyndrach's log book, which lay on the hood of the dashboard.

"The sun that put Asgard through the warp might have gone out," I said, "but there are fusion reactors down there that are still working. There's heat down there, and life too—but it's not quite what anyone expected to find."

15

Her eyes narrowed, and she said: "What exactly is in that notebook?"

"Just the log of Saul's last journey," I answered, deliberately offhand.

"When I say 'exactly,'" she said stonily, "I mean *exactly*."

"I'll make a deal with you," I offered. "You tell me why you're hell-bent on catching Myrlin, and I'll tell you what's in the book."

"You don't make deals," she told me. "You follow orders. I'm ordering you to tell me what's in that book."

I thought about digging my heels in. What was she going to do—hold a court-martial and have me shot for insubordination? I decided to be generous, though. There's no point in trying to fight personal wars out in the cold—you can find trouble enough without making your own.

"Saul found some kind of dropshaft," I said. "He worked his way down to the bottom using ropes. Once there, he didn't have the equipment he needed to cut his way out, but he did manage to drill a peephole. On the other side, there was light and there was life. The temperature was above freezing. He couldn't see much, because there were walls in the way—the building housing the shaft was in an advanced state of dilapidation, but its structure was still sound. He saw plants, and insects of some kind, but he couldn't see out of the window because it was blocked. There was no sign to suggest that people had used the building recently. Everything not made of stone seemed to have rotted."

"And that's where Myrlin's gone?"

"He's got drilling equipment with him," I said. "They ordered it on my phone. But once he's through, he might have an entire hollow world to hide in. Assuming he can find the head of the dropshaft. That's not going to be easy even for us, and we have detailed written instructions. First he has to get down to four, then he has to undertake a long trek through the cold. He's had no experience out there, and he'll be relying on a verbal account given to him by a dying man. He might not make it. If he does make it, then he might well be able to find another shaft that will take him even lower. Heat and light need power—somewhere down there machines are still working, including a reactor of some kind. That implies that there are people. If so, then our days of scratching around just beneath Asgard's skin are over, and we can solve all the puzzles I was telling you about."

"They might not be people," she said. "Not humanoids, that is."

"All the stuff we've been digging out of the top levels is designed for the use of creatures pretty much like us," I told her. "There's no doubt they're humanoids. Some people—the ones with the wild imagination—think they may be *the* humanoids."

"I don't get it."

"In the part of the galaxy we know about there are maybe a thousand humanoid races. They all come from earth-type worlds, and they're basically similar both physically and chemically. Most theorists figure that it's a matter of convergent evolution—that nucleic acids are the only molecules that can serve in reproductive systems, and that the evolutionary sequences which produced us all have some kind of inbuilt determinism, so that they differ only in detail. Beings like us, it's argued, are the only kind of beings that can acquire our kind of intelligence. Those non-humanoid races we've come across are also stereotyped in their own way, and they tend to come from a set of worlds where conditions are similar—though by no means Earthlike. The minority report, though, holds that all the humanoid races are similar because they all have a common ancestor—that life came to all potentially Earth-type planets from some kind of independent source. Some argue that the basic chemical systems which are necessary for life evolve in interstellar dust clouds, and that they seed all the likely environments with the same starting material. Others argue that the seeding was done deliberately, by conscious beings duplicating their own evolutionary processes. Because no one knows where Asgard came from, or how long it's been here, it makes a convenient home for the hypothetical proto-humanoids."

"It seems to me," said the star-captain, "that people feel free to make up just about any story they damn well like. All this is pure fantasy."

"That's exactly right," I told her. "The center of Asgard is the perfect imaginative space for setting any kind of mythology at all. While no one knows what's down there, *anything* is possible. In some ways, that's the main attraction of the place. There's a sense in which salvaging the technological gadgets from the cold is only a rationalization of what we're *really* doing here. What we're *really* doing is confronting a mystery. Everybody loves mysteries. Everybody *needs* mysteries. Humans call the planet Asgard because that's as close as we can get to providing our equivalent to the name the Tetrax have given it. Asgard was the home of the Norse gods, but the Tetron word doesn't quite imply 'home of the gods'—it means 'the essence of mystery,' with 'mystery' being construed in a metaphysical sense. Most of the people here have a burning desire to get as far into the heart of the planet as possible, because they're half convinced that what they'll find there is something that will transcend all worldly ambition, something that will give them a special and vital insight into the way the universe is put together. A million other projects on a thousand other worlds probably have similar significance for the people involved with them. Ever since we stopped believing in God, we've been trying to find a substitute."

"It seems to me," said Susarma Lear, who was by no means the last of the great romantics, "that you're all crazy."

"Probably," I admitted.

"Until you read that notebook," she said, "you had no reason to think that there *were* any levels beneath those you'd already penetrated. Even now, there may only be ten or twenty. There might just be a single deep cave. All this stuff about an artificial sun in the core, attended by the race who created all the humanoid species in the galaxy, is a fairy tale fit for children."

"Maybe," I said cheerfully.

"You don't believe any of it," she accused. "Not really."

"It's not a matter for belief," I told her. "It's all conjecture. A bagful of dreams. But you can take dreams seriously. Dreams really *deserve* to be taken seriously. Maybe they're the only things that *are* worth taking seriously."

"I still say you're crazy."

"To tell you the truth," I said, "you don't seem so completely sane yourself. This obsession with hunting androids doesn't seem altogether healthy, and your secretiveness about your reasons is positively paranoid. What the hell has he *done?*"

She turned away to stare out into the black night.

"He—it—hasn't done anything," she said, in a dead tone. "It's what he might do, given the chance."

I couldn't help feeling that her attitude said far more about her than about the android. It seemed to me that she was—in some weird way—punishing *herself*. Heaven alone knew why.

It was a mystery to me.

16

I was still driving when the sun came up, though the star-captain had gone into the back to get some rest. Serne had replaced her, and was getting ready to replace me at the wheel.

When the rim of the sun suddenly appeared, as a slowly expanding yellow arc away to our right, he drew his breath in sharply. There had been a silver glow in the sky for some little while, but this was different.

The sunlight spilled across the plain like a flood, turning the dead-white carpet of snow into a sea of glittering gold. The sky lightened from jet black to a deep, even blue, uninterrupted by the slightest wisp of cloud.

Serne shielded his eyes, and tried to look out into the glare, to watch the fiery crescent ascend into the blue, but he couldn't bear the glare.

I took a pair of sunshades from the pocket beside me and passed him a second pair.

"Don't look directly at it," I said. "It'll blind you."

"It's so *big*," he whispered.

"It's larger than the Earth's star," I confirmed. "Asgard is closer to it, as well. But it's partly an optical illusion caused by the snow reflection, and by the fact that it comes up so slowly. Asgard doesn't turn very fast. Wait until you see the sunset—there's a lot more vapor in the air then, and it turns the whole damn world into an ocean of blood for more than an hour."

He looked out across the illuminated plain, seeing it for the first time. It was still featureless, and would be until the snow melted and exposed the shallow undulations and the vegetation. It seemed to go on forever, and must have seemed unnatural to him—he was used to trees and hills and all the things which break up a landscape and give you the chance to get everything in perspective. Here, there were no bench-marks, and distances seemed somehow unreal. It was as though we were heading through a kind of limbo.

I called through to the other truck, and told Crucero to put on the shades. He reported that everything was satisfactory, and made no comment on the beauty of the sunrise.

"Maybe the captain should take a look?" I suggested to Serne.

He shook his head. "I think she's sleeping. You don't wake a star-captain to tell her the dawn looks pretty."

I shrugged. "Have you served with her long?" I asked.

"A while," he said uncommunicatively. "It's been a long tour, with our finally getting to make the landing and all."

"You were part of the invasion force?" I asked.

"It wasn't really an invasion. We pounded hell out of Salamandra from space—the battle in the system must have lasted a solid month. We went down to mop up after the barrage was over. There wasn't a lot left."

"You came to Asgard from the battle zone, then?"

"That's right," he said. "Another job to do. Mopping up."

"Why is it so urgent for you to catch up with this android?"

His face never seemed to change expression. He talked in a low, flat voice, his brown eyes never settling. He seemed to be looking at me now almost for the first time, from behind the protection of the shades.

"He's dangerous," he said laconically.

I got the impression that pressing the point would be rather unwelcome. I shut up. Surprisingly, he went on: "If the star-captain wants you to know, she'll tell you. Don't try to put pressure on."

"Yeah," I said. "She acts as though she's been under a lot of strain lately."

"You don't know what the hell you're talking about," he answered, in a tone that suddenly sounded almost threatening. "Don't push things with her, or with anybody. Don't try to be so clever."

I didn't reply to that. There didn't seem to be anything much worth saying. But there was something more that he wanted to get off his chest.

"I think you ought to know," he said softly, "that if anything you do causes trouble for the captain, you're going to end up very dead."

Having said that, he went back to staring straight out of the window. I wondered just how many crazy people there were on this expedition. There was something more in Serne's devotion to his senior officer than a proper respect for military discipline. It wasn't too hard to see why. There were probably nearly as many women as men on the ship that had brought Susarma Lear to Asgard, but there wouldn't be many women among the combat troops. Star-captain Lear was rather special—who else would Serne and his fellow troopers fantasize about while they were screwing members of the technical staff or jacking off? Troopers can't screw captains, but they can dream. And what else is worth taking seriously?

"Are you from Earth?" I asked, feeling that our relationship ought to be put on a rather friendlier basis.

"Space-born," he replied tersely. "In the belt."

"I was born in the belt myself," I told him. "My father came from Canada—went out to the belt to build ships. In the end, he shipped out as part of a diplomatic mission to establish relations with the Tetrax. We didn't get to see much of the Tetrax, though, being ship's crew. That was where I heard about Asgard. I came out here with three other guys nearly ten years ago. The others are all dead now. They got killed in a darkside accident. I wasn't with them—I was minding the store in Skychain City. I nearly gave up and went home, but somehow I kept missing the ships that were headed for Earth."

"You missed the war," he said. His voice was level, but somewhere behind the words was a criticism.

"Yeah," I said tiredly. "I missed the war."

After a pause he said, "They never got to Earth. The belt wasn't so easy to defend. Must have been more than a million people in the belt. A hell of a lot got killed. Everyone *I* ever knew, outside the force."

"I'm sorry," I said.

"They paid for it," he assured me. "We damn near wiped the bastards out."

"So I heard," I said dryly.

"You maybe think we shouldn't have?"

I shrugged. "I don't know how the war started, or why."

"And you don't care?"

"I care."

He deliberately looked the other way, out across the glittering plain, as if he were trying to lose himself in it. He seemed to me to be already lost. I think he felt that way, too.

Before I went back into the body of the truck to sleep, I gave Serne careful instructions on the use of the direction-finding equipment and the map showing the watercourses. I wasn't altogether happy about trusting him, but with the star-captain watching over him I assumed that he wouldn't dare to make a mistake. I was sure that she, at least, was competent.

The general idea was that we would keep going, driving in shifts, hoping to catch up with Myrlin before he got to the surface-point where Saul had gone underground. He had a long start on us, but presumably he had to sleep and eat. What would happen if we *did* catch up with him on top, I wasn't quite sure, but I was convinced of one thing: I wasn't going to turn around and go back once the star-force had got their man. I was going to follow Lyndrach's route all the way to the end, whether it upset the star-captain or not.

By the time I woke up again, the sun had actually cleared the horizon, and it hovered above the eastern horizon looking as if it might fall at any moment and burn us to a crisp. The snow was showing no sign of melting—its glittering surface reflecting the light rather than absorbing it. Under the influence of the light the canopy of the truck had grown dark and smoky, but it was still necessary to wear the shades.

As Serne made his way back to the bunk, I took the passenger seat beside the star-captain.

"Anything happen?" I asked.

"We got a call from the ship. A few hours after we left the city, a convoy of trucks came out of the same lock. They're following our course, straight as an arrow."

"It doesn't surprise me," I said.

"What are we going to do about it?"

"Not a thing," I told her. "Not until we're underground, anyhow. Then we'll see about getting rid of the bugs they're using to track us. For the time being, let them think they have us where they want us."

"There is an alternative," she said.

"Go on," I said. "Surprise me."

"My ship is armed with orbit-to-ground missiles. We could wipe them out with one strike."

"I don't think the Tetrax would like that," I said gently. "They'd be inclined to look upon it as an act of barbarism. The war's over, remember. You can't spend the rest of your days shooting up other people's planets."

"So what could they do?" she asked, lifting her hands off the wheel for a moment. "Are they going to take on an armed ship? With what?"

I shook my head slowly. "Even if they couldn't do a damned thing," I pointed out, "it would foul up communication between our two species for a century or so. In fact, I think you'd find that they could pull the teeth of your warship without too much trouble. You'd find yourself in exactly the same mess you pulled *me* out of back there, and half your crew with you. The Tetrax don't go in for fighting, but they're not too fond of people who try to fight against them. If we have to stand and fight it out with Amara Guur, let's do it privately, down in the cold. Discretion pays, believe me."

She shrugged her broad shoulders. "All right," she said. "We'll do it your way. But no petty gangster is going to interfere with our business. If he takes it into his head to pick a fight with the star-force, he'll regret it."

That was comforting to know. I thought so, anyhow.

I asked if I could fix her something to eat, but she refused. I got my own breakfast, and ate my way through it slowly.

"Hey," she said, when I'd finished. "How far down do you think we'll have to go, when we get to this place we're going?"

"Saul doesn't say," I answered. "Don't worry, though—we won't be going all the way to the planet's core. There isn't a rope that long."

"How many levels do you think there might be?"

"The radius of the planet is about ten thousand kilometers," I said. "If it really is made up entirely of hollow shells, there could be fifty to a hundred thousand of them. Nobody knows, yet. All we know is the overall density of the world, which is a little over three-and-a-half grams per cubic centimeter. It's bigger than Earth, of course, though its surface gravity is much the same. We don't know how to interpret that density, and we don't know whether it's uniform all the way down—most likely it's not, of course."

She was silent for a few moments, and then she said: "If the radius of this world is half as much again as the radius of Earth, it must have more than twice the surface area. If there are only fifty levels, each one with no more than half the area of the surface, that still means that there's as much space inside as there is on the surface of fifty whole worlds the size of Earth."

"That's right," I agreed.

"How many people would it take to do a building job like that?"

"A lot," I answered. "If they're all still around, down below, they must be pretty crowded. In evacuating the surface and the top four levels alone, they've effectively evacuated seven or eight times the surface area of Earth. That could run to billions of people. That may be why they wormholed the whole world —if they *did* come here from the black galaxy—instead of taking the population off in smaller ships."

She fell silent again, thinking it over. I knew that the moment she started playing around with figures she would start falling for Asgard's mystique. It was beginning to make itself clear to her just how much there might be hidden under the surface.

"Are there any Salamandrans in Skychain City?" she asked suddenly.

"I don't even know what one looks like," I said. "Those are the people we were at war with, right?"

"Right."

"Why do you want to know?" I was tempted to add some sarcastic comment about hunting them down to the very last man, but thought better of it.

"I was wondering why the android came here."

"The Salamandrans would know about Asgard, even if none of them were ever here," I pointed out. "They must have made contact with the Tetrax, just as we did."

"Maybe it just seemed to him to be a likely place to hide," she said.

"Maybe," I echoed. "As you just pointed out, where else can you get fifty worlds for the price of one? It's the greatest place in the galaxy to get lost."

I refrained from adding that if that *was* his intention, we'd never find him. The last place he'd go would be where Saul Lyndrach told him to go—unless, just possibly, he figured that might be his only way down to levels where there was light, and life, and breathable air. I didn't want to say any of that out loud because I thought there was a possibility she'd go on talking.

"On the other hand," she said, "he might be looking for something."

Aren't we all? I said to myself silently.

"Tell me," she said, ruminatively, "do the Tetrax know how to clone individuals of other humanoid species? Could they make a hundred copies of the android, if he could persuade them to do it?"

"I guess they could," I answered. "They can certainly clone themselves. You think he wants to turn himself into an army of supermen? To wreak vengeance on the human race on behalf of the Salamandrans who built him? I'm not sure the Tetrax would be party to a thing like that. In fact, I'm sure they wouldn't."

She stared at me from behind her dark glasses, and I couldn't tell what kind of expression there might be in her eyes.

"He has to be killed," she said. "I want you to understand that. He really does have to be killed."

"Sure," I said, through gritted teeth. "I really do get the message. I really do. I just don't see what the hell he can *do* against the whole bloody human race."

This time, though, her silence was a kind of retreat—a withdrawal into some private area of her consciousness, where she could sit and lick old wounds in psychological peace.

I guess that taking part in the murder of a world is the kind of thing that can leave something of a bad impression on your memory. A little bit of her, at least, was still in a state of shock.

18

Two days out we had to bear eastward to skirt the southeastern arm of one of the northern hemisphere's larger seas. It had hardly begun to melt, and the bergs still stood up like a row of jagged teeth against the horizon, gleaming where they caught the sunlight that flickered over them. For a while, it made a pleasant contrast with the featureless plain, but in its own way it was just as boring.

"Is it all so goddam flat?" growled Serne, in one of his rare communicative moments, when the two of us were sharing the cab.

"Pretty much," I told him. "There are clusters of buildings scattered all over the world, but no substantial conurbations. It seems that people worked up here, but they didn't live here. When they took their leave, they took virtually everything they could carry—they left far less machinery here than in the lower levels. We figure they retired underground to live a long time before they retreated from the levels. Mostly, they used the surface of the world for growing things—or so we think. There's not much evidence of solar-power equipment or anything of that kind. Virtually all the shaping seems to have been done in order to control the movement and distribution of water. We should pass the C.R.E. dome soon, though. That'll break up the tedium of your day."

"Is that where we're going?" he asked.

"Hardly," I said. "The C.R.E. doesn't allow independent operators to use their routes. The cave-system on level one is arrayed rather like the petals of a flower, with a series of arms radiating out of a central hub. The hub of this system is a long way north. The C.R.E. has a dome there, and so does one or two of the independent concerns, but it's really too far away from Skychain City to be convenient. The dome we'll see is on the arm closest to the equator. Saul will have poked around until he located a way down into one of the other arms, near enough but also far enough away. He won't have built a dome, of course—just a hole with a plug in it. Not even a beacon to draw us to it. Without knowing the location given in the book —and equipment good enough to get an accurate fix from the satellite—no one could find it. Myrlin probably parked my truck a couple of miles from the hole and pulled a sled across the snow from there. We'll probably arrive soon enough to follow the tracks, but a snowstorm would wipe them out. It doesn't bother us, of course—but it might make a big difference to anyone following us."

Personally, I was praying for some foul weather before the thaw really set in. Guur might be able to figure out where we were in the levels, if his bug wasn't completely screened by the surface structure, but figuring our position wouldn't be the same as figuring out how we got there. On the other hand, finding our trucks would be child's play, and all he'd really have to do would be to wait, if he had the patience.

"What kind of power-unit do the sleds have?" asked Serne.

I laughed. "Muscle-power," I told him. "Where we're going, it can get very cold. Machines don't work too well down in three and four. It's not absolute zero, but it's near enough. The atmosphere is pretty thin, of course—most of it has liquefied out or frozen—so it isn't as if you're totally surrounded by cold. It's like being in space, in a way—except for the soles of your feet, and your gauntlets, every time you touch something. You can't take any kind of wheeled vehicle down into the levels. I've heard that C.R.E. has had some limited success with hovercraft, but hovercraft have to settle when they stop, which means that you have to erect some kind of dome-bubble every time you put the brakes on. C.R.E. goes in for bubble-building in a big way, but we don't. The organized crews tend to work slowly—essentially they're *repossessing* parts of the lower levels, building insulated structures and boosting the temperature inside to something tolerable. Their exploratory ventures are short-range, tentative forays. Operators like Saul and me work in a different way. We *move*, as fast and as far as we can, covering the territory in the hope of running across something new. We use trucks on top, sleds on level one, but below that we walk, and hope that the men who made our boots and gloves weren't telling lies about the tolerance of their materials. Gas-packs keep us in air for twenty to thirty days at a time; everything is chemically recycled. The main input is carbohydrate. On a trip, we lose weight and our digestive systems get thrown out of gear, but we recover."

He turned his bleak eyes on me, and I realized I'd let my mouth run away from me. I wasn't talking to some immigrant who'd come to Asgard from a colony world, looking for an easy way to make a fortune. I was talking to a starship trooper, who'd probably lived in a spacesuit just as long as I'd lived in a cold-suit. He knew about the physiological effects of minimal life-support as well as I did, and at least I had the benefit of knowing when I was out on a long tour that no one was trying to flame me down or hit me with a particle beam.

At least, I had always had that advantage before.

"I'm sorry," I said. "I guess you've already had your fill of suits and gaspacks."

"We only use heavy suits where there isn't any atmosphere," he said colorlessly. "Most of the *real* fighting is done on worlds where the temperature is fine and the atmosphere is breathable —except for biotech weapons. Mostly, we wore sterile suits like glorified plastic bags, that didn't slow us down. They hug your skin, and thin as they are they still have networks of ducts that carry your sweat away. Before you put one on you have to shave all over, and then they shoot you full of some inhibitor that won't let the hair grow for a while—except that it does, just a little. Just enough to make you itch, until you feel that your skin is crawling. You can't scratch—not properly. You spend your days and nights moving about under a blue sky, or under the stars, with growing things all around you, and sometimes cities that you could mistake for any place on Earth, but still you're in your suit, because the air might be filled with human-specific infective agents. Ninety percent of the time, of course, it isn't . . . but you have to wear the suits anyhow, living by courtesy of the machine in the middle of your back. The suits are practically indestructible—they can't tear no matter what you do to them—but somehow you never feel safe touching anything. And the machine's on your back where you can't see it and you can't touch it, masterminding your chemistry like a little god. Somehow, the middle of your back seems more remote than the ship, more remote than the stars in the sky."

If he'd stopped halfway, I'd have told him that I understood —that I knew how he felt. He went on long enough, though, to convince me that I didn't. His was a special paranoia.

I'd wondered, once or twice, whether the star-captain and her merry men could handle themselves in the lower levels. Now I decided that they probably could. In all probability, they could handle themselves there a great deal better than Myrlin, or anyone in Amara Guur's party, despite the fact that they'd be working a strange environment and wearing cold-suits for the first time. If they decided to stay, and go into competition with the C.R.E., they might make quite a team, I thought.

"Having had it that bad," I commented, "I'd have thought you'd head straight for home now that the war's over, instead of coming here."

His lips seemed hardly to move as he said: "It isn't over."

He seemed to be telling me that the whole human race was now at war with one lone android.

A special paranoia, indeed.

19

My truck stood in gracious isolation on the empty plain. The snow had barely begun to drift around its wheels, although there was a keen wind blowing from the nightside toward the hotspot where the sun stood at its temporary zenith.

"Look," I said to the star-captain, "we could be in trouble here. Some time, we're going to have to come up again. We can't hide the trucks. When we *do* come back, we might have to fight to get back inside. I don't know how many men Amara Guur has, or how many he'll leave here, but I know they'll be waiting for us."

"I can still have his convoy blasted," she said levelly.

"No," I answered. "The only thing we can do is to inform the Tetrax what's happening. I want to make sure they know—and that Guur knows they know—exactly what's going on here, as far as the Lyndrach notebook is concerned. What happens below the surface is something they can't control, but I want Guur to know that anything which happens *up here* is under observation. I think they'll be willing to take such steps as are necessary to make sure of that—after all, there are a lot of murders tied up in this matter already, and the Tetrax are jealous of their ability to maintain law and order."

She shrugged. "Go ahead," she said. "I don't want to get shot as soon as I poke my head back out of this hole of yours."

I had to get her approval before I put the Tetrax fully in the picture. There was, of course, a corollary to their making sure that anyone who murdered us on surface would get theirs in return, but I didn't want to spell it out for her too explicitly, in case she changed her mind. The corollary was, of course, that if Myrlin returned to the surface, *she* wouldn't be able to kill *him* without getting hers in return. The moment Myrlin came through Immigration Control he was under Tetron protection, and the Tetrax weren't likely to make any special exceptions for assassinations supposedly carried out in the line of military duty.

I called the satellite, gave them my position, and told a Tetron peace officer the story of Saul Lyndrach's notebook. Needless to say, he was annoyed with me, though he was far too polite to show it. He pointed out to me in gentle terms that the right thing to do would have been to surrender the notebook the minute it came into my possession, explaining all my theories about who had murdered whom *then*. I pointed out, in terms equally reasonable and modest, that I would then have lost the chance of making a bid for the center, and that my main interest for the present was in preventing further crimes. We could all join together in the investigations pending, I suggested, once we were all safely returned to Skychain City, by which time I hoped to have occasion for further celebration by virtue of having found a way to the planet's core.

I think the officer understood my point of view. He reminded me of a few technical offenses I was committing, but he didn't bluster or threaten or order me to desist. Nor did he promise to make sure that a benevolent eye would watch out for my eventual return to the surface, but I got a distinct impression that it would.

I have no proof that Amara Guur was listening to what we said, of course, but radio waves are free—anyone who can intercept them is surely entitled to decipher such information as they are carrying.

"All right," I said, when it was finished. "Now we can go."

We left only one man in charge of the two trucks—Trooper Vasari. Five of us set out in cold-suits to follow the tracks of Myrlin's sled across the melting snow, with drilling equipment and everything else that I thought we might need temporarily lodged on a sled of our own. The star-captain and her bravos wore their flame pistols outside their cold-suits. I did wonder, briefly, whether flame pistols would work at ten degrees absolute, but I decided that they probably would. If there's one thing that we make well enough to operate under just about any conditions that are conceivable, it's weaponry.

It took the best part of an hour to reach Saul's hole. Even without the dead-reckoner and Myrlin's tracks, we'd have had little difficulty finding it. Myrlin hadn't bothered to re-plug it, and it was there for all to see: a jagged-edged pit. Saul had obviously blasted it out.

Places where the surface is thin enough to blast or drill through are not exactly common on Asgard. There are no roads leading from one level to another via gently sloping tunnels. There are whole sections, sometimes twenty or thirty meters across, which once went vertically up and down, slotting neatly into the profile of both levels, but they tend to be several meters thick, and they fit very securely. C.R.E. and like concerns have managed to put one or two back into working order, but such sophistications were not for the likes of Saul Lyndrach. What he (and I) habitually looked for were places where there was a nice thin hatchway intended for the use of individuals. I suppose there must have been millions of them dotted over the planet, but they were still hard to locate and identify, and they were scattered far and wide. Saul was always good at finding them. A good knowledge of the geography of both the surface and level one, together with a lot of logic and a little intuition, helped him a lot, but he had a little extra touch of genius too. Saul Lyndrach found more ways into level one from the surface than anyone else on Asgard. The big teams, of course, found far more—but they usually found them the easy way, from underneath.

Getting the sled down to level one took another hour; getting the equipment and ourselves down took another. Myrlin had left one of his own cords secured to the rim, but I left it alone and secured my own. The cord, of course, was biotechnological "rope," compounded out of monomolecular strands of a very tough protein. It wasn't phenomenally strong, though it would do all the jobs I wanted it to, but the best thing about it was that it didn't mind cold in the least. It was also thin—between us we were carrying several million meters of the stuff.

Most of the way down we were descending through a narrow

vertical tunnel. There had once been a ladder of sorts, but corrosion had got at it long before the cold stopped the rot—probably while it was still in use. On level one, chemical processes had been operating again for a long time, and now for all practical purposes it was an ex-ladder.

Eventually, the tunnel became a wall, or rather a covert that was almost semicircular in section. We were in a kind of alcove, with a large open space before us.

The first one down was Lieutenant Crucero, who found that his searchlight—mounted on the crown of his helmet—was just powerful enough to pick out the other wall running parallel to the one in which our alcove was set.

"Where are we?" he asked. We were keeping an open channel on the intercom, so everyone could hear and speak to everyone else. He looked at me when he spoke, his searchlight dazzling me. That's one of the worst things about working with a team in the levels—people instinctively look at you when they speak to you, and if you happen to be looking at them, it can cause a good deal of mutual inconvenience.

"According to Saul," I said, "we're on one of the main arterial highways in this particular network. It's about the luckiest strike you can get. There are hundreds of branches within striking distance of this point, and each branch has sub-branches . . . and so on. From this one point, a lone operator can go to any one of ten thousand places where he might find dropshafts to the lower levels. If you come down in a sub-sub-branch, you don't have anything like that kind of choice. Of course, a man could spend a lifetime exploring the neighborhood and still miss the one thing he'd most dearly like to find, but Saul had a nose for opportunity. I don't know how often he'd used this hole, but he can't have been working it more than a year—maybe eighty days down under. Without knowing where to look, we could all die here without getting close to the vital spot."

"Are you sure you have those directions correctly memorized?" asked Susarma Lear.

"Lady," I said, "I've been doing nothing else while you and the trooper were driving the truck, except perhaps sleep once in a while. I've been rehearsing the route even in my sleep. It's not my memory you have to worry about—it's Saul's. Theoretically, he should have been talking into his recorder every step of the way, and the notebook should only be a written version of that record, but I know only too well how easy it is to forget to mention something while you're wandering around with your mind on what you're looking for."

We didn't start out immediately—not until I was sure that Vasari could cover the hole adequately, to screen it from searchers. When he went back to the trucks, he could sweep up our tracks, too—but he couldn't really conceal them without help from the weather. Maybe we could buy time that way, maybe not, but I wanted to be certain that we did what we could.

When I was sure, we set off—following the road northwestwards.

We didn't talk much, though Crucero did ask at one point why the road was walled in on either side. I pointed out to him that the walls were helping to hold up the roof. He shut up then, feeling like a fool.

The outer levels of Asgard were built upward, one on top of another, but in many ways they appear to have been constructed the other way—as if the natives had started at the surface and excavated each level as a series of cave systems. There aren't very many open spaces where the surface is supported by pillars—the living space is all tunnels and enclosures; wherever you are there are always walls close at hand. Sometimes those walls are very solid—their thickness varies from several meters to several kilometers. The material they're made out of varies in texture; sometimes it's stony, sometimes it's more like plastic. Its density varies too—obviously the variation has something to do with the fundamental structure of the whole artifact, though it hasn't been well enough mapped for us to understand the pattern in its entirety.

The highway itself was empty. The layer of ice that dressed it was very thin—not much water found its way in here, and the temperature was high enough for all the atmospheric gases to be gaseous—but the surface was smooth enough for the sled to go over it as easily as we could wish. Periodically, we saw some of the vehicles that the indigenes had used on the road in the unimaginable past, but they were just heaps of slag by now, parked in neat rows in wide alcoves, sometimes partially screened from the road itself.

"How do you ever manage to recover anything worth having from *those?*" asked the star-captain, after pausing to inspect one.

"We don't," I told her. "It's next to impossible to find anything worth a damn on level one. The best things come from three and four, where time has virtually stood still since the cold first wormed its way down there after the big blackout. Hardly a molecule has stirred, even in the millennia since the heat of the sun has percolated back down there. Since *we've* been here, of course, the process has accelerated a bit, but outside the little bubbles the expeditionary forces bring down with them, everything is still in suspended animation."

Most of the side branches we passed were open, but I ignored them. There was no time for curiosity. We had to travel a long way northeastward before we reached our own turnoff. The only things I made a point of looking for were Saul's flashmarks, where he'd torched some kind of a mark on each of the turnings he'd investigated. There were usually two marks—one made going in, the other coming out; the second ones were code-symbols reminding him of what he'd found. Each trip would be fully logged in the earlier part of the notebook—probably in earlier notebooks, too—but there had to be some kind of reference-point down here. I couldn't read the code fully, though I knew what one or two of the symbols stood for, and could make reasonable guesses at most of the others.

We took turns hauling the sled, and after a couple of hours on the road we took a rest. The troopers seemed to be taking it all in their stride. There were no complaints. I felt as uncomfortable as I usually do, with sore patches where the suit's systems were plugged into my body at the neck and the groin. It always takes a day or two to strike the new balance. You can't just switch over to being a cyborg by the act of plugging in. You have to undergo a more gradual process of metamorphosis.

By the time we stopped a second time we had virtually lost contact with Vasari. There was too much insulation blocking out the carrier wave. It would have been pleasant to imagine that Guur might also be losing contact, but I knew that his tracking bug would be more sophisticated. We might even be leaving some kind of evident trace—at least, the star-captain might. My main worry wasn't to do with the bug *she* was carrying, but more with others that I might not know about. There was always the possibility that he'd somehow managed to secrete one in the equipment we had, at source or during delivery.

After a while, the silence began to get on our nerves. Serne and Khalekhan began to ask trivial questions just for the pleasure of hearing their own voices. I realized that it must breed a special kind of patience to be on long missions communicating through a wide-open intercom channel, so that every word the troopers exchanged their officers could overhear. It put a different light on Serne's habitual taciturnity.

"The territory on either side of the road along here," I told them, in response to one question, "is farmland. The farming's mostly hydroponic, of course, so what you'd see if we followed a branch would be vast mazes of ice-filled channels. The lighting equipment is all derelict now, of course—so is the harvesting equipment. No sign of life, either, though there are probably spores in store and in the ice that would germinate if conditions ever became right. The Tetrax have restored some of the equipment under Skychain City to provide food for the immigrants, but it wasn't just a repair job. They had to replace virtually everything except the basic structures. They feed the power downward, of course. The natives maintained some power supplies on this level, but they fed nothing down from the surface. Apparently they had no solar cells on top, and no satellite power stations beaming microwaves down. Their main supplies always seem to have come upward. In a way, that's natural—these levels were built outward one at a time—but it also implies that deep down inside there's a very powerful energy source. Or was, a few million years ago."

"I take it that we're heading for a town?" asked Khalekhan. "That's where we'll find a way down to the next level."

"That's right," I told him. "At least, it's a town in the sense that there were once people living there. Not a major center of population, though. It's more a kind of industrial estate—a complex of automated factories. There were permanent dwellings there, but nothing like the kind of thing you find in the cities at the hub of each complex. We're still a long way out on the arm here."

"If your ultimate objective is to find shafts that go a long way down," the star-captain interjected, "wouldn't you be most likely to find them in the hub of the complex?"

"If the cave-systems were stacked one on top of another like a pile of pennies," I said, "that would be the natural assumption. In that case, one could imagine elevator shafts connecting the whole sequence of cities from top to bottom. Unfortunately, they didn't build that way. The hub of each complex tends to be set above a solid mass. The reasons are presumably macroarchitectural, though some people think the cavies simply liked it that way. What we have here isn't something akin to a gigantic inverted skyscraper with each floor corresponding to one of the levels. The natives weren't in the habit of commuting regularly from one level to the next, and certainly not from top to bottom. Each level, you see, is independent in the sense of being a coherent, closed ecological system. By ecology, I don't just mean biological ecology, I mean politics and economics too. The complexes didn't have to trade with one another—each one, if it wanted to, could be a completely self-sufficient world of its own. There *was* communication between levels—at least, there exist facilities which would have made such communication possible—but they didn't build these complexes on the assumption that a large fraction of the population would be perennially moving up and down, or that manufactured goods would be moving up and down in any great quantity. The one exception, as I've said, is the matter of the initial energy-input. Each complex had generating facilities that were probably adequate to keep things going day by day, but we think there's also a supply that they drew on routinely which pipes energy up from below—not from the next level, but from some system which is embedded in the macroarchitecture itself—something which originates below *all* the levels, in the center."

"You keep working your way back to that hypothetical internal sun," observed the star-captain.

"Yes," I said. "Yes I do. I think it's there, and I think it's still blazing. Somewhere beneath our feet—not too far down, if Saul's log is to be trusted—there are complexes which can still draw on that common energy source. They were far enough away from the surface not to have to compete with the freezing effect of the cloud. That's probably not very deep—hardly any deeper than the colony worlds have to go in order to mine coal —but to get there we have to cross the final circle of Dante's hell, and so far no one's found a direct route. No one, that is, except Saul Lyndrach."

"But you could be wrong," she pointed out. "Even if Lyndrach's right, and some kind of life does survive in one complex down there—it may simply be a single self-sufficient complex. There's no guarantee that there are vast inhabited realms below it."

"Sure," I agreed. "Anyone can be wrong. Every single one of the thousands of people who swarm down the skychain in search of miracles could be chasing a mirage. But then again, we may be right, and Valhalla may be just beneath our feet."

20

We slept that night in hammocks slung from plastic frames, which touched the ground only at the tips of their four feet. This, at least, was something that was new to the troopers. At least the kind of hells *they'd* been through were places where you could throw your sleeping bags on the ground. In level one, of course, we could have done that—but down in the lower levels it pays to be more careful. The cold can't hurt you if you're insulated from its grip by a meter of quasi vacuum, but once it gets you into its clutches, it can be difficult to break free.

We reached our turnoff early next "morning," and it was something of a relief to be able to turn aside; it gives one the impression that one is actually going somewhere when there is a genuine corner to turn.

I checked the symbol that Saul had used as a flash-mark to indicate the beginning of this particular journey. There was no second mark to encode a reminder of what he'd found. He wouldn't have needed reminding, if he'd been able to return.

There *was* a second torch-mark, though, higher up on the wall. It was just a simple curlicue, but its presence was oddly unsettling. It wasn't Saul's—it had to be Myrlin's. He hadn't put it there for his own convenience. It served no useful purpose. In its own enigmatic way, it was a kind of message. It said: "I know you're going to see this. I don't know who you are but I know you're coming after me. Don't expect to find me unprepared."

I didn't bother to translate the message for Susarma Lear. I don't think she noticed the flash, let alone read any particular significance in it. I suppose I should have told her, just as I should have told her about the bug Jacinthe Siani had managed to plant on her in the Plaza back at Skychain City, but two things stopped me. One was the fact that she wouldn't tell me all *she* knew about who and what Myrlin might be. The other was the fact that I was determined to play a lone hand all the way through this crazy business. *She* might think that I was a trooper in the star-force, but I was still of the opinion that the conscription papers I'd signed didn't really mean a thing. After all, I *hadn't* killed the Sleath, and Tetron law, despite all its pretensions, was barbaric in its insistence on selling people into slavery. As long as Susarma Lear had those conscription papers, backed by the force of Tetron law and Earth law alike, she could hardly be reckoned to be friend rather than foe, and her fight wasn't my fight until she was prepared to prove to me that it had to be.

By the time we stopped to sleep again we had made the second turning, and were less than a kilometer short of the point where the straight tunnel would break up into a web of capillary tunnels. Here the going would get rough, because we'd no longer be following a road built for vehicles, but corridors built for pedestrians—or, sometimes, for small monorail trains. Eventually, it would be the monorail which would guide us to our way down to level two.

"How much farther?" asked the star-captain. "Until we reach this shaft that goes down as far as the light, that is."

"We won't make it tomorrow," I told her. "The day after, if nothing goes wrong. Tomorrow night should be the only one we have to spend in the cold on the way in. Saul spent six days down there finding the way for us, but we'll only need one to follow it. We won't stop to load up, either—he probably moved a few things around, to make it easier to pick them up on the way out. Now get some sleep. We don't have time to waste."

"I think we ought to post a guard," she said.

"I don't," I told her. "If each of us stands guard for a hundred minutes, that means the total time we spend here is a hundred minutes longer than it has to be. We all need eight hours' sleep, and we all need to make the very best use of the time when we're *not* sleeping. No guards—they'd be wasting their time. Are you worried about the android attacking us? Or about the possibility that I might run out on you?"

"Both," she said.

"In that case," I said, "you wouldn't want me to stand guard anyhow. I'm getting eight hours' sleep. If you think that your men can get by on six, you're welcome. If it were my decision, I think I'd save my energy, at least for a couple of days more."

I didn't bother to stay awake to find out whether she did post guards. If she did, she gave the orders by sign language. I kept the intercom channel open.

The next day was a long, hard one, but I had to admire the way the troopers handled conditions on two, and the way they worked to keep the sled going. Working the levels isn't something that most men can take to readily. The least trace of claustrophobia shows itself by the third day, and any anxieties about the dark you might have can build up into real paranoia in that time. I expected the troopers to get jittery because they had manifest paranoia already built in, but they kept calm. Apparently, the knowledge that for once they weren't surrounded by enemies was all the comfort they needed. Despite the captain's statutory caution, they weren't really scared of the android—yet.

Serne did say to me at one point that he didn't see how a man could wander around in such an environment for twenty days and more, on his own, without going crazy, but I assured him that with a little practice, solitude wasn't too hard to bear, and that the black-and-white surrounding eventually got to be just like home. I didn't tell him that I usually brought an earplug with three hundred hours of talk and music in its microtapes, with a blink-controlled on/off switch—somehow it would have sounded like a confession of weakness. After all, it wouldn't be the kind of thing a man could carry into battle, would it?

The conversation flowed much more easily now—partly because we were getting to be a little more comfortable with one another's presence, and partly because we were relying more and more on the auditory environment to fix our attention. They'd grown bored with looking around them, and the things they saw had stopped acting as a spur to the imagination. They needed some kind of stimulus input to keep their minds in trim, and talk was the best supply we had just then. Most of what we said was functional talk—or, at least, talk that pretended to be functional, but eventually we began swapping anecdotes.

I told them about working the caves; about the kind of things I'd found, and about the kind of things it would be good to find if luck went my way. They told me about fighting the Salamandrans, and how they'd avoided getting killed. I guess their stories were more exciting than mine—some of them would have curdled the blood of a lesser man.

"This may seem like a stupid question," I said, at one point, "but what exactly were we fighting the Salamandrans *for?*"

"We were trying to colonize the same region of space," said the star-captain. "Between us, we were virtually surrounded by other cultures longer established in space. We had settled neighboring worlds—sometimes we made agreements that allowed us to settle the same worlds. That was the fatal move. In making it we thought we were cementing an alliance between our species. For a while, we made a fetish of cooperation, thinking that it proved the value and the workability of the brotherhood of species. We were wrong. The closer we worked, the worse became the friction. In the end, we found that we were *too* close. When hostility began to build, it couldn't be contained or diverted. There wasn't any one incident that can be said to have caused the war—just a process of positive feedback that magnified trouble and kept on generating more. By the time the bombing started, there was no way to stop. It was simply a matter of going all out to win, because there was no guarantee that anybody not on the winning side would survive. There was too much at risk for anyone to play dove—the only way to be sure that the human race had a future was to make sure that the human race won the war."

"Isn't that rather a dangerous way of thinking?" I asked.

"Sure it's dangerous," she told me. "It's all very well for bastards like you, hundreds of light-years from the nearest fighting —and your Tetron friends—to disapprove, and to reel off all the usual cant about having to live together eventually, but you haven't had to go to sleep every night for more than ten years with the possibility that you might wake to find the whole world turned into slag by Salamandran bombs. Maybe we could have avoided the war if we'd been able to draw up a stricter division of the worlds we wanted to colonize, but we didn't know that at the time. Interracial cooperation may seem easy enough on a world like this, where everyone lives amicably under the kindly eye of the Tetrax, but isn't that really because no other race is strong enough to challenge them and because no group of races could muster the mutual loyalty necessary to oppose them?"

"The people at C.R.E. seem to get along well enough together," I pointed out.

"But they're an organization of volunteers, aren't they?" she observed. "If they weren't committed to getting along, they wouldn't join. What percentage of the men working the levels actually work for the C.R.E.? Suppose they were all *compelled* to work together in the same organization?"

"Nobody likes being compelled," I told her. "By their own kind, or by any other. That's not the point. The point is that most spacefaring humanoid species manage to get along without having to blast one another out of existence."

"There've been interstellar wars before," said the star-captain, darkly, "and there'll be others in the future. I hope *we* don't get messed up in any more, but I don't think that's something that can be determined entirely by our efforts. If we do get involved again, I don't think any way of thinking is likely to get us out except the way that got us out this time. Always provided that we're fighting someone our own size. If we're not, then no way of thinking is going to help."

I couldn't help feeling that she was just a little too dogmatic in her assertions, and I knew full well that her way of thinking could be dangerous for *me*, but there was no point in pushing the argument. I left it there, and didn't even bother to inquire again about Myrlin's place in her scheme of things. If she was ever going to tell me, she'd have to do it of her own accord.

We finally stopped for the night in a kind of amphitheater that might have been used for sporting contests of some kind, or dramatic performances—or maybe even for something that had no close parallel in our terms. The route we'd been following passed alongside it, but it seemed somehow more suitable to sleep there than in what was effectively just a glorified corridor.

Relative to the hub of the particular complex we were in, we were just about in the same position we'd been in on level one —except that the hub was in the opposite direction. We were some way out along one of the arms, in a township gathered around a series of factories. It was the kind of place where I'd expect to find a route down to three or four without too much difficulty, but if Saul's log spoke the truth we wouldn't have to wander around in four—we could go all the way down from three.

When I went to sleep that night, I dreamed about that descent. I had dreamed about descents a dozen times before, and in substance this was no different, but there was a fervor about the way I moved through the uncertain chain of scenes that was new. It wasn't a good dream, and it came to nothing—as all such dreams come to nothing—but it was far from being a nightmare. Without being in the least prophetic, it was very much a dream of anticipation.

21

Down in three I expected to find much the same kind of territory as in one and two, but I was wrong. There was no factory complex, just a series of "fields," with the characteristic grid pattern of hydroponic cultivation. The route which we followed between them wasn't a road but a monorail track, where automatic trains had distributed seed to the planting machines and collected produce from the harvesters. Sometimes our view was blocked by a wall on one side or the other, but there was usually open country either to our left or to our right.

There was enough space for the sled to move beside the single rail, and we walked there too, though there was a thin catwalk beside the track intended for the use of humanoid beings.

Periodically, we passed machines that once had tended the things which had grown where there was now nothing but ice. They looked very different from the cars we had seen beside the highway up at one. There had been little or no corrosion, and where the metal and plastic *were* pitted the damage was hidden beneath a sheen of ice which shimmered in the light of our lamps. Once we had to work our way past a train abandoned on the rail. All its cars were empty. It was an obstacle that caused us some problems, because it was difficult to get the sled around it. We had to unpack the gear and then repack it all again, and it all took time that I begrudged.

"It's weird," said Crucero, while we were working there. "It looks as if it could just take off again, as smoothly as you like, if the current came back on. It seems as if you'd only have to switch on the lights and this whole place could come to life again."

"Things have deteriorated more than it appears," I reminded him. "The upper levels have been exposed to processes of decay for a long time since the sun began to shine again on the surface, but three and four have escaped that. You still have to take into account the deterioration suffered before the cold closed in, though. I don't know how much time elapsed between the day this level was abandoned and the day the temperature reached its present economical standing—it probably wasn't all that long, by comparison with the time that the surface and one have been warmed over again—but it's not just time that's important. When this place was constructed it was designed to be permanently energized. It wasn't intended to be switched off—ever. Parts of it, no doubt, would have to be taken out of commission in order to effect repairs, but there was no provision made for a total shutdown. Getting it back into working order isn't just a matter of throwing a switch. Nothing much happens to a big brute like that train if it lies idle for a few days or a few years, but for the control systems it's a different story. They're too delicate to tolerate alien conditions for long."

"You said that the Tetrax had restored some parts of the top level," said the lieutenant.

"Sure," I said. "They've made the food-producing system produce food again. But it wasn't just a matter of switching back on, and what they've put into operation is *their* system, built on the skeleton of the one the cavies left behind."

We went on, heading the way the train had been pointing. There was no special significance to that, but it seemed somehow to be a hopeful sign.

If the lights *had* been on, we would have seen our destination from a way off, but when you're traveling with the aid of searchlights built on to your helmet you're restricted to a sensory environment no more than thirty or forty meters across, whether you're completely hemmed in by walls or not. We passed the yards where the monorail trains had discharged their cargoes in some unbelievably distant past, and found ourselves in a small complex of corridors and cells. The main doorway to the complex must have been closed when Saul first found it—he'd forced his way in with the aid of levers and a torch. He'd paused to torch his mark onto the wall beside the door, but there was no corresponding mark higher up. Myrlin had already made his point.

Two things struck me about the complex as we began to work our way through it. The first was the density of doors. The cavies didn't go in much for doors, except in their actual dwellings. When you live underground, in a perfectly regulated environment, you don't need doors except to secure privacy—or secrecy. There probably was living accommodation in the complex somewhere, but the doors we were passing—and sometimes passing through—weren't that kind of door. They were big, and close-fitting. The other thing that I couldn't help observing was the kind of hardware that was built into the place. In the rooms that Saul had opened up there were no bare walls. Everything was storage space of one kind or another—for objects or for information. There were display screens and other data facilities, but not in any overwhelming profusion. There were also big steel boxes that might have been refrigerators, irradiation chambers or ovens. More significantly, there were big transparent plastic bowls, completely sealed, equipped internally with systems of robot hands.

They were like nothing I'd seen before on any of the levels. "We're in some kind of lab," observed the star-captain.

"That's right," I said. "Biotechnology of some kind. Lucky Saul. Even without the dropshaft, he'd have been able to mine this place for years. There must be a lot of stuff here worth salvaging despite the fact that they stripped it when they left."

"How do you know they stripped it?" she asked.

"They stripped *everything*," I told her. "All they left for us was their litter, and a few things they couldn't be bothered to take. What they could use, they took." To emphasize my point, I jabbed a finger in the direction of a wall which had a section of floor-to-ceiling shelving. "Empty," I said.

"Where's this shaft?" demanded the star-captain.

I shouldn't have needed reminding.

"I don't know," I told her. "The instructions run out here. All I know is that it's here. It won't be difficult to find. Even an expert cracksman like Saul couldn't batter his way through every door in the place."

We moved on, taking care not to pass any open doors, whether they'd been broken open or had stood open for millions of years. I was possessed by an urge to start opening *more* doors, and breaking into cupboards, searching out the hoarded goods that must be there, but I kept it under control. There would be time.

There was just one place where I lingered, letting my curiosity off the bit, and that was beside one of the transparent chambers. Inside it, there was an assortment of equipment—tubes, pipettes, reagent jars—and with them a sealed metal canister. I couldn't see any seam by which it could be opened, but there had to be one. I could hardly help wondering what was inside it. If I'd been able to find *that* out, I'd probably be halfway to figuring out why, in this place but hardly anywhere else in the upper levels, there was an elevator shaft that went a long way down: not just to four or five, but to forty or fifty, or maybe to four hundred or five hundred.

In the end, it was Serne who found the shaft. He called out to us to come quickly, and we all followed the customary pantomime of asking "where?" so that he could reply "here." You don't get much idea of distance or direction over an intercom link, so we all had to work out our own way of finding him.

If we had been in any doubt whether Myrlin was still ahead of us, what we found in the shaft settled the question. There were two doubled-up cords secured at the top. Saul would only have used one. Even more significant as evidence was the air current that was coming up the shaft. We couldn't feel it, of course, but we could see its effects along the corridor which led to the shaft. We took measurements of pressure and temperature once we got the sled in, and they confirmed that this was one little corner of level three that was warming up a lot faster than the rest. It wasn't exactly tropical yet—it was a hell of a chimney that the air was climbing—but it was no longer the next best thing to absolute zero. Saul, according to the log book, had only drilled an itsy-bitsy hole at the bottom of the shaft, but the current coming up the shaft wasn't from any pencil-thin jet. It looked as if we weren't going to need to do much cutting and hacking ourselves.

"I'll say one thing for friend Myrlin," I said. "He sure can cover the ground. Doesn't he ever sleep?"

"I don't know," murmured the star-captain. "But we can't be far behind him."

"It's going to be a long ride down to the bottom," I said, changing the subject. "We should rig up some kind of cradle, and a scaffold so that we can let ourselves down the middle of the shaft instead of having to brace ourselves against the side wall. The temperature's probably high enough to let us operate a block-and-tackle without the pulley freezing solid, especially if the man who stays up here can keep it in order. It won't be the same as the original elevator, of course, but it should be a more comfortable ride than Saul or Myrlin had."

"Who's going to stay here?" asked Crucero.

The star-captain looked at me.

"Oh no," I said. "You need a man you can trust—a man with a gun. Suppose the android gets behind you and comes back up the shaft—you'd need someone here who could take care of him."

She told Crucero that he could stay. I think he had mixed feelings about it. He was curious enough, in his way, about what was down below, but it didn't mean as much to him as it would have if he'd been on Asgard for years instead of a few days. To him, the center was just another place. He'd have liked to be down where there was light and air, instead of being alone in the cold, but that was all there was to it.

"They also serve who only stand and wait," I assured him. But to him it wasn't a joke.

"Let's get to work," said Susarma Lear.

We began preparing for our descent into the abyss, and our passage from the seventh circle of hell to the prospect of paradise.

I am not by nature an optimist, but this time I really did think that I was on the road to a kind of paradise. The mythology of the center had that firm a hold on me.

As I think I've said before, anyone can be wrong.

22

There was another dispute, of course, once we'd rigged the scaffold and were ready to start lowering our first ambassador to the world below. I wanted to be the first one down, but I was overruled. After some argument, Serne was given the job. The star-captain graciously agreed that I should go third, ahead of Khalekhan. This did not reflect my own idea of my importance, and it also meant that I had to spend a lot of time waiting at the top of the shaft when I might have been exploring at the bottom, but the star-captain was in command.

"What happened to the elevator itself?" asked Crucero, as we began the long task of winding Serne down into the darkness.

"Good question," I said. "Maybe what's left of it is a tangled heap of scrap at the bottom. More likely, it's the roof of the elevator where Saul finally ended up. The shaft might go on almost forever."

There was no cable in the shaft, and no mechanism in the crown from which a cable might have been suspended. Instead, there were ridged grooves on each side wall into which the elevator had slotted, though it wasn't immediately obvious how it had been powered or secured.

"If there really is a way past the floor that Saul found," I said, more to myself than to the others, "and the shaft really does go all the way down, this is the doorway to everywhere. All of Asgard is ours. I wonder how long it will take us to explore it. . . . I'll bet you could lose the entire human race down there."

Even as things stood, of course, there had to be doors that would open onto other levels—probably to every single level between here and the level where life still thrived.

If the Tetrax find out about this place, I thought, *they'll probably install a turnstile. Asgard's own inbuilt skychain.*

I was still hoping, of course, that a complicated miracle might hand the whole thing over to me. There was an alien android ahead of me, and the vormyr behind me—not to mention the star-force all around me—but there was still a sense in which I felt that the moral entitlement was mine.

But we do not, unfortunately, live in a morally-ordered universe.

It took a *long* time for Serne to reach the bottom. Finally, though, he announced that he had arrived.

"What do you see?" asked the star-captain tensely.

"Walls," he replied laconically. "There's mold, or something like it, growing all over them. The door closing off the shaft is metal—it's thick, but it's only some kind of light alloy. The android seems to have cut his way through without too much difficulty; the fused edges are slick enough. The outside's corroded, but it's covered by the same kind of stuff as the walls. The light's dim—it's not coming from any kind of bulb. Some of this mold is luminescent, but in here it's only twilight. I can see the way the android went out. He's left his cutting gear here."

"Stay where you are," ordered the star-captain. "I'm coming down."

We linked up the second cradle, and began to wind it down with the captain inside. As it descended, the cradle Serne had used began to come back up again.

"Can you see any sign of human habitation?" I asked of Serne.

"Human?" he queried.

"Let's not split hairs," I said. "Is there anything to suggest that anything looking like you, me or a Tetron has set foot where you are in the last few million years?"

"There's nothing," he assured me. "Just different kinds of mold. Of course, it may be different outside."

"You stay put," said the captain quickly. "Don't move until we're down."

"Sure," said Serne. No other thought had crossed his mind since she'd first issued the order. There was a pause, and then he added: "You're wrong about the elevator. No wreckage, and the floor of the shaft is absolutely solid. Hard as rock."

I frowned, and looked again at the grooves in the side walls, wondering if I could possibly have misinterpreted them.

"I can understand them taking their lab equipment away," said Crucero. "But why would they take the elevator out of the shaft?"

I didn't have an answer to give him.

"Isn't this rather a weird place to put an elevator anyhow?" asked the lieutenant, when he saw that no answer to his first question was forthcoming.

"Maybe," I said, not wanting to jeopardize my reputation for infallibility any further.

"Don't jerk that cord!" snarled the star-captain.

While the captain was making her slow descent into the unknown I looked pensively at Crucero.

"Look," I said, "I'm not sure it's such a good idea for you to stay here. I don't know that Guur's men *can* track us through the levels, but if they do, you'll be in bad trouble."

"Leave that to the lieutenant," the captain interrupted. "He knows what he's doing."

Crucero made a sign with his hand, indicating that the star-captain was right and that he did indeed know the score.

"I don't intend to fight it out," he said. "If they show, I let them through. I'll take care of anyone they leave behind. That way, no matter what happens downstairs, nothing and nobody comes back up without my saying so."

"Mightn't that leave us four intrepid explorers a little exposed?" I inquired.

Again he made a dismissive gesture with his hand. Obviously, a star-captain and a brace of troopers armed with flame pistols were expected to be able to handle a few petty gangsters.

"Do you want a gun of your own?" asked the lieutenant.

"I don't have room in my belt," I replied dryly. It wasn't just a joke. I was carrying a good assortment of tools.

I followed Susarma Lear down the long drop as soon as she signaled that she'd reached bottom. I stopped worrying about such stupid matters as military tactics and concentrated on more important issues—like the possibilities that awaited me at the lowest level ever reached by any member of Asgard's legions of scavengers. This was what I'd been living for during the hardest years of my life, and even if circumstances weren't quite as my dreams had imagined them I was damned if I was going to forgo the luxury of savoring my good fortune. I pictured myself as the very archetype of Faustian man, about to come by the knowledge and wealth for which I would gladly have traded my soul. The sweet taste of that illusion made irrelevant the fact that I would still need one hell of a lot of luck to avoid ending up in hell.

The room—if you could call it a room—into which the elevator shaft opened at the bottom was a sad disappointment. As Serne had said, there were walls and there was mold. Once that was said, he'd just about run through the inventory. The only thing I could get excited about was the fact that opposite the door to the shaft was another door. It was shut, or at least pushed to, but someone had cut out the lock. All that it needed was a good shove. Myrlin, I decided, must have had a tidy mind. Anyone else would have left it yawning open.

I went to give it the shove it needed, but the star-captain ordered me to stand still and wait. Khalekhan was still in the shaft. I knew that the minutes which had to pass before he appeared were going to seem like hours.

I looked down at the floor of the shaft. I was still using my headlight—the bioluminescence of the mold wasn't sufficient to see by. Serne and Susarma Lear still had their lights on, too. Serne had been right about the solidity of the floor. We certainly weren't standing on the roof of the elevator. The grooves which I'd taken to be the beds for the elevator's lifting mechanism continued all the way to the floor, and looked as if they disappeared straight into it.

"Okay, wise guy," said Serne, when he saw what I was doing, "where's the remains of the cable? Not to mention the cage?"

"I don't think there was a cable," I told him. "As for the elevator itself, it's down *there*." I pointed at the floor.

"That's solid," he observed.

"Pretty solid," I conceded. "But it's a plug nevertheless. For some reason, they sealed the shaft. Naturally, they sealed it with the elevator on the underside of the seal. You can tell it's a plug by the way it joins the wall, especially at the grooves. There's an evident meniscus, where they made certain of the seal with some kind of hard-setting liquid."

I could feel my heartbeat as I followed the train of thought along. *Here,* they'd sealed the shaft. Here and nowhere else. Why? The explanation that sprang most readily to mind was that this might be the last of the abandoned levels. Valhalla might be just beneath our feet. I was tempted to get down on my hands and knees and put my ear to the ground, just in case I could hear the murmuring engines of a thriving civilization.

"If the light outside is no brighter," mused the star-captain, "there isn't going to be much here in the way of wildlife."

"It seems silly to waste our efforts in conjecture," I said, as much to myself as to her, "when the answers are so close at hand—and waiting for us."

There was no arguing with that, and so we simply stood and fretted until Khalekhan arrived, keeping our fantasies private. When he *did* arrive, there was a further pause for military ritual, as the *real* members of the star-force checked their guns and confirmed with empty gestures the commonalty of their cause. Strangely enough, I didn't really mind the further delay, because it seemed that there was a certain propriety in the fact that there *was* a ritual. This was a solemn moment, and needed to be treated with respect in order to be properly charged with meaning.

"All right," I said, when the star-captain seemed ready, "I go first, right?" I tried to sound authoritative, as though it was only natural that I should lead. There was probably a small vestige of humanity left somewhere in the core of her being, because she simply waved me on.

23

I stepped across the threshold between the worlds without much difficulty. The door yielded easily to the pressure of my hand. I wasn't surprised to find myself in a corridor. It seemed logical enough that there'd be some kind of establishment here similar to the one at the top of the shaft. *This* corridor, though, was very much warmer than the one up above, and like the room we'd come from it was dimly lit by bioluminescence. The beam of my light picked out scuttling white insects, which rapidly disappeared into various nooks and crannies. There was nothing more exciting than that.

I checked the temperature, and found it to be two-seven-six absolute. Three degrees above freezing. Not comfortable, for the insects, but tolerable. The fact that the shaft was open probably meant that there'd been a considerable drop in the local temperature. Outside the establishment, it would probably be a lot warmer.

I led the way along the passage, following the traces left by the giant android as he'd scuffed away the thin organic slick that covered the floor. We passed through two more doorways, each one opened by sheer brute force and left open. It wasn't until we reached the main door that we found more evidence of cutting and of tidiness. *This* door opened inward, and I had to lever it with my own cutter. So far, we'd seen virtually nothing of the establishment itself—not enough to decide whether it was a lab complex or a laundry—but there'd be plenty of time. My one thought was to get *out*, into the cavies' version of open territory.

As I levered back the door, I held my breath, and when I moved through I exhaled very slowly. I may have made some meaningless and irreverent remark—I really can't remember.

There was more light outside—diffuse white light that seemed to emanate from everywhere: from a mottled "sky" that seemed oddly like an Earthly sky thrown into negative, with a silver background interrupted by black "stars"; from the ground that glistened as though it were the skin of an adder or a colorless frog, likewise dappled with grey and black; and from long cobweblike strands that festooned the "trees" and "bushes."

Though there was more light, the suggestion was still of night rather than day. Without our headlamps we would still have been able to see, but not well. Even *with* the aid of our lamps it was as though we had come into a world of shadows.

We were confronted by what I can describe only as a forest, though the "trees" were not decked out in green leaves. No doubt there *were* photosynthetic organisms here, but they were clearly unimportant members of the ecosystem. The energy which fed the continual metamorphoses of this alien flesh was almost certainly heat diffusing from below, and I guessed immediately that there must be more than enough of it.

There was a tree-branch near enough to touch, and I did so, sweeping aside a few gossamer-light bioluminescent strands. The dark branch was rigid but brittle; it broke easily. Its texture, as I crumbled it in my gauntlet, reminded me of fungal chitin.

I had little opportunity for a fuller examination because our light beams were attracting small flying things in great quantities—they were like tiny moths with black and white wings, and they gathered in such a swarm that it was barely possible to see through the crowd.

Susarma Lear swore.

"Switch off!" she commanded. We complied, and moved away from the doorway to escape the living cloud. The trees did not have canopies borne aloft on stalks so that it was easily possible to walk beneath their spreading foliage. Instead, they were rounded, elliptical in vertical section, often supporting a halo of undergrowth. There was little in the way of bare ground—or, rather, ground carpeted by a relatively thin encrustation of fungoid life. This might be an easy place to get lost, but it would also be an easy place in which to track an enemy.

"Look," said the star-captain, pointing upward into the middle distance. There we could see other flying things, plainly much larger than any insect could be, gliding and flapping furiously between the conical crowns of the trees. Some shone faintly, either with light of their own or because they had dressed themselves with strands of the ubiquitous bioluminescent mold.

"I think I know what's happened here," I said, as I began to step farther ahead of my companions, trying to drink in everything that was there to be seen. I never got to show them how clever I was, though, because I was interrupted.

Inside the suit, of course, I could hear no noise from outside. Suits designed for work in a near vacuum don't have pick-up mikes. The first warning I got, therefore, was Serne's cry of alarm when he made eye contact with the thing. By that time, it was already charging.

It was coming from the right, and considering its bulk it was accelerating very nicely. It probably weighed about twice as much as I did, and simply for that reason I wouldn't have liked to have it collide with me. When I took in the spikes on either side of its snout as well, I quickly came to the conclusion that I wanted to be out of its way. Unfortunately, cold-suits aren't designed for sprinting. I set off at right angles to its path, but it veered around to follow me and the distance between us was being eaten up with every second that passed. The damned thing was no more than a meter behind me when the beam from Serne's flame pistol licked out to fry its brain. Even then I had to sidestep to avoid being hit—it had built up a lot of momentum, and its legs were still going like pistons.

"Thanks," I said to Serne. He didn't reply. He was half crouching, his gun weaving a slow pattern in the air as he searched the shadowed trees to his right. Susarma Lear and Khalekhan had their guns out, too. They had formed a triangle, and were covering sixty degrees apiece, as though they expected a horde of naked savages to come hurtling out of the bushes at any moment. The way they handled themselves, any gambling man in the galaxy would cheerfully have laid out a thousand to one against the horde.

I knelt over the body of the animal. Its skin was smooth and hairless, but thick and tough. Its feet were small, with three toes aggregated into a kind of hoof. Its forequarters were massive, and its ridged spine had a kind of frill or fin along most of its length. It didn't have much tail. The spiked snout was long and rounded, and the mouth underneath was filled with big, squarish grinding teeth, except for a few incisors at the front.

I have no experience of alien ecologies, but I do know something about the range of humanoid species, and the kind of ecological factors that are responsible for the differences between them. I could read a couple of interesting conclusions from looking at the creature's makeup.

Susarma Lear finally convinced herself that no other frightful alien menace was about to descend upon us, and came to stand beside me.

"You want to go back for a gun?" she asked.

I nodded slowly. "We'll have to get Crucero to send equipment down the rope anyhow," I said. "There must be worse things than this down here."

She didn't have to ask why. The spikes on the snout weren't for decoration, and the fact that the beast had been programed to charge implied that there were other beasts it *had* to charge. The way it carried its head and the teeth that filled its mouth made it obvious that it was no hunting carnivore itself.

"Considering that this is an artificial world," observed the star-captain, "the inhabitants certainly don't make much effort to keep things looking nice. And what pets they have, hey?"

"The ecology on this level's run wild," I said. "That's why it was sealed off. Each cave-complex must have had a closed ecology when the whole world was working properly. Everything balanced. When the exodus began, and the upper levels had to be evacuated . . . you can imagine how easily the balance might be upset. It should have been possible to correct an upset, but maybe the circumstances wouldn't permit. Maybe it was simply easier to evacuate and seal the complex. *That* must have been a livestock species once. That bioluminescent stuff was probably engineered specifically as a light source. One thing we know for sure is that this level wasn't abandoned recently—and by not recently I mean that we're talking about millions of years. This lot didn't evolve overnight."

"That doesn't tell us anything we didn't know already," pointed out the star-captain.

I didn't like the way she kept putting me down. On the other hand, though, it did ease my conscience regarding the fact that I was still planning to desert.

"I'll tell you one thing *I* didn't know," I said. "There's still some kind of energy input to this complex. Something's sustaining the life-system, and it's maintaining a stable temperature. This little baby isn't insulated to conserve its metabolic heat—quite the reverse. Unless I'm mistaken, that frill along its back can be extended and engorged with blood in order to *lose* excess heat. That suggests that keeping warm is no problem."

"So?" she said.

"They switched off the power to the upper levels," I said. "They could have switched it off here, too—but they didn't."

"Maybe they forgot."

"Sure," I said, trying to sound utterly unconvinced.

"This isn't getting us any farther forward," she said. She turned to look for the other troopers. While we'd been chattering, Serne had been looking around. He'd found Myrlin's trail, and drew our attention to it. He pointed away into the wilderness, but mercifully refrained from saying, "He went thataway."

Khalekhan, meanwhile, still had his gun in his hand, and was patiently vigilant.

"Let's get back inside," said the star-captain. "We get the stuff down; we rest—and then we move."

I looked down at the marks made by Myrlin's boots. They were quite distinctive—nothing like the track the animal had left when it charged me. Maybe out *there*, though, there'd be animal trails that were well-enough used so that he could follow them without leaving a distinctive track. Maybe there'd be bare ground. Surely there'd be water. He could slip us easily enough, *if* he knew he was being followed. I wasn't even sure of that—maybe he underestimated the obsessiveness of the starforce.

Later, when I strapped on the flame pistol, somehow making room among the clutter that already dressed the outside of my suit, there was actually a moment when I felt like a starship trooper, fearlessly treading alien soil for the everlasting glory of Old Earth. The feeling wasn't as bad as I might have anticipated.

But it was bad enough.

24

There *was*, as I had anticipated, water. In fact, there was much more of it than I had anticipated, and it looked *evil*.

Myrlin's trail led us straight to it, no more than six units' march from the bottom of the dropshaft. Maybe once it had been a hydroponic farm or a system of reservoirs. Now it was a swamp whose waters were stagnant and soupy, with drifting mats of vegetation, small islets crowded out by skeletal dendrites decked with shiny tinsel, clouds of flying insects and rising bubbles of marsh gas.

"Pity we forgot the boat," I murmured, as we stood contemplating its dim-lit vastness. Our eyes had accustomed themselves to the twilight by now, and we had been able to see well enough so far, but the swamp looked worse than the "forest."

"Trooper Rousseau," said the star-captain coldly, "you're not funny."

"No," I admitted. "It's my one enduring fault.

"We're beat," I went on, when she didn't reply. "We couldn't track a bulldozer across that. He's lost, for once and for all." I tried to sound regretful, but it wasn't in me. The thrill of the chase was all very good, and so far it had taken me more or less where I wanted to go, but that little game was all played out as far as I was concerned.

"Follow me," said Susarma Lear, in her most determined tone. She sounded as though she were chewing on ground glass. She was out of her mind, but I hadn't the courage to tell her so. She walked slowly into the water, testing its depth as she went, simply heading in the direction Myrlin had been going. She was no more than thigh-deep when the bottom leveled out, and there were obvious signs of disturbance in the fibrous rafts ahead of her, once we got close enough to see.

I sighed, and ploughed on, reassured that even if I went out of my depth I couldn't drown. As long as my cold-suit was intact, *nothing* could happen. Even while I was reassuring myself, though, I began to wonder what the creatures lurking down below might *do* to the suit while they had uninterrupted access to it. The possibility of getting wet feet was too dreadful to contemplate. I didn't want to spend the rest of my life in a place like this.

It wasn't much comfort to me when my prophecy finally proved correct beyond a shadow of a doubt. We *did* lose him, and ended up ten or twelve kilometers out in the swamp, without a clue which way to go. We hadn't been following a straight course for some time, but zig-zagging from one trace to another. There was no way we could know whether all the traces—or, for that matter, *any* of them—had been left by Myrlin.

We stopped to rest when we came up against an expanse of open water. We couldn't see another shore, and without the islets dressed in bioluminescent tresses there was no way to estimate its extent.

"Face it," I said, trying to sound soothing, "your wild geese have flown. We can follow our own trail back—I've made sure of that. It's all we *can* do, now."

"And what do we do when we get back?" asked the star-captain, sounding extremely unhappy.

"You can wait for him in the hope that he comes back," I said. "Maybe you can bottle him up here forever. What *I* intend to do is find some kind of road or railway—what's left of it —leading away from that installation. Once upon a time, there were cities here. I want to find the cities, and I'm not going to do that by wandering around this festering swamp."

"You're forgetting something, trooper," she said. "Your days as a scavenger are over. You're in the star-force now. You take off on your own, and that's desertion. That means that if you ever surface again, you're in *deep* trouble."

The thought *had* crossed my mind. But I also knew that if I got out of this place, I'd have marketable knowledge that could tempt even the Tetrax. No one on Asgard was going to hand me over to the star-force while I could be useful to them here. It was up to me to cultivate my usefulness as much as I could.

What I said, however, was simply: "All right, Captain—what do *you* suggest we do?"

"We go back to the edge of the swamp," she said. "And then we go around it. He had to come out some place, unless he's still here."

I began to shake my head in mixed disgust and despair. Then I stopped, as my eye caught a movement in the black lake. It was only a ripple, rolling in toward the shore, but it was a big one.

"*Captain*," whispered Serne, who had seen it too. He was drawing his gun as he spoke.

It drifted slowly into view, preceded by more ripples, and for a moment I breathed a sigh of relief. It looked flat and glassy, and glowed very faintly, and could easily be taken for a raft of vegetation. The only thing was that there was no current for it to be drifting on. It had to be moving under its own power. Khalekhan had raised his gun, but now he relaxed and lowered it again. Serne, by contrast, took aim. He was blessed with an innately suspicious mind.

I watched the thing grow in size as more and more of its bulk was forced out of the water, and I realized that it wasn't floating at all. It was oozing along the bottom, and all we could see was the tip of the berg. Its surface was semi-transparent, and the tiny pinpricks of light were *inside* it rather than encrusting its surface. It resembled nothing so much as a gargantuan blob of protoplasm—an amoeboid leviathan.

Even after I realized that, it *still* took me by surprise. Somehow, unthinkingly, I imagined it as being rounded, but of course it wasn't. The tip-of-the-iceberg metaphor didn't begin to suggest how big it *really* was. The pseudopods were out of the water and flowing around our ankles while its "head" was still thirteen meters from the shore.

My instinct was to flee, and I danced backwards away from groping jelly. It was like trying to jump out of a stream of treacle, and I nearly fell, but my reaction was the right one. Serne's reflexes were geared up a different way, and the moment he heard my horrified curse he let fly. A tongue of red death spat out at the protruding mass, which seethed and boiled as the beam cut into it. But there was no brain there to be fried in its bed, and there was no nervous system to communicate the fact of death to the whole creature. The coenocytic mass simply *split* along the line of the beam, rolling back from its deadly touch. Two more beams licked out, moving like slicing blades, but *this* beast didn't mind in the least being sliced, and the glu-

tinous, gleaming grey gel flowed up the legs of the intrepid sol-
diers of Earth.

Up and up and up.

I ran, stumbling through the shallow water as fast as I could
go—faster, at any rate, than the lake-dweller could possibly
follow.

There was screaming ringing in my ears—not screams of
agony or anguish, but the sound of sheer panic. There was no
way I could tell which of the three had given way, finding himself (or herself) in the grip of some preternatural nightmare,
because the sound blotted out any saner voices that might have
tried to intervene.

After thirty seconds, without any promise of abatement, I
could stand the sound no longer, and I switched the radio off.
There was nothing easier, then, than simply to keep going. I
was alone, and I was free. Their game, as I had told them, was
over, and all that was left was to play my own.

The only trouble was that in the urgency of my flight from
the lake monster I had come away from the blazed trail that I
had been careful to leave behind our little expedition. When I
began to look around for islets where I had been careful to
leave evidence of our visit, I could not find one, and in searching I must have blundered too far in the wrong direction.
Without realizing, I turned myself around once too often, and
was hopelessly lost.

I swore at myself, and then set about calming myself down.
When I was sure that I could trust myself again, I set out in a
randomly chosen direction, trying to hold to it as best I could,
and blazing a *new* trail so that I would know if I circled back
on myself. It was only a matter of time before I reached the
edge of the swamp, and I was safe if I kept my wits about me
and sidestepped any further encounters with the sinister inhabitants of the region.

To keep myself company, I tongued in the music tape that I
had set up in my helmet ready for my desertion from the star-
force cause. It helped to steady me, not because of any quality
inherent in the music, but because it restored the familiarity of
the situation. I was alone, in semi-darkness, beneath the surface
of Asgard—and that had become, over the years, the existential
condition of the real me. I began to feel more confident, and

even cheerful, though I remained just as watchful as humanly possible.

I didn't think about the beautiful star-captain and her faithful followers. I blotted them out of my consciousness as if they had never existed. It wasn't so much that I was heartless enough not to care what had happened to them—it was simply that I couldn't *afford* to care; not then, and not consciously. Eventually, I knew, there would come a time for remorse, and guilt too, but for the time being it was as if I were alone in the universe, with no connection with or responsibility to any other living thing.

Another twenty-five units passed before I reached the edge of the swamp, but my dead reckoning never played me false. Maybe I didn't keep straight, but I didn't circle either, and I was eventually able to pull myself up a muddy slope to a long, narrow ridge which skirted the marshland. I knew before I reached the top that I was onto a winner, and I wasn't surprised when I got there to find the remains of the rails. They had what I guessed to be millions of years of rust on them, but rails they were. I looked one way along them, and then the other, and then I began to walk, ready to keep going until exhaustion set in.

The pipes kept pumping nourishment into my bloodstream, and carrying the wastes away. The suit kept the oxygen flowing into my headspace, purged of carbon dioxide and other poisons. The music washed my auditory canals like a drug, soothing and balancing, and anticipation grew.

When I first saw the hulking shadows of buildings beside the line, I thought for a fleeting moment that it might be the city I was looking for, but the softly shining wilderness still stretched without interruption to either side, and I knew that it was only a way station. Still, it promised a place to sleep that would be as safe as anywhere—walls from which to sling my frail hammock.

The place was just a ruin, as I had known it would be. Anything and everything that had been abandoned there had long since decayed into utter anonymity. Even the walls, though they had been built of a substance their builders must have considered well-nigh indestructible, were beginning to crumble.

I was not dissatisfied; I knew that my time must come. I simply made ready to sleep, in my customary calm and efficient fashion. If I had bad dreams, they were gentle enough not to wake me, or disturb my memory.

25

I was used to sleeping alone—alone, that is, in the sense that under normal conditions I pitched my hammock in total darkness, in temperatures a few degrees above absolute, confident in the knowledge that the nearest human being was probably thousands of miles away. Because of that, I was usually a fairly sound sleeper. I could afford to be.

Though the circumstances of the present trip—and, more especially, of the present moment—were far from normal, I hadn't managed to adjust the physiological habit of several years. I slept the sound sleep of the innocent and trusting. All of this I mention to account for the annoying fact that while I slumbered unthinkingly on, someone contrived to remove the flame pistol from my belt without so much as causing me to stir. I didn't even *begin* to wake up until the thief started tapping on my faceplate with the barrel.

The first thing I focused on, naturally, was the shadow of the gun. Then I looked up. The weak bioluminescence was behind him, and from my viewpoint his helmet was just a big black blob, but I didn't have the slightest difficulty in recognizing him.

He was *enormous.*

When he was sure that I could respond, he began moving the point of the gun-barrel over the faceplate again—not tapping this time, but spelling out a series of figures. He only had to repeat it once before I realized that it was a code frequency. He was telling me to readjust my radio. I did as I was told.

"Hi," I said, to tell him that the task was complete. I didn't want to say anymore. The floor was his.

"Mr. Rousseau, I presume," he said. I nearly giggled, but it was natural—no joke.

"You can call me Mike," I said. "We haven't been properly

introduced, I know, but we have exchanged a few brief words on the phone. Sorry I couldn't put you up—I seem to have caused you quite a bit of trouble, one way and another."

"Quite all right," he assured me. "After all—think how much less convenient it might have been for both of us if you'd been showing me the sights of Skychain City when the star-force arrived."

"Yes," I said. "But I sure as hell wish you'd been with me when Balidar hooked me into that damned card game." I paused reflectively, and said, "You know I brought the star-force with me, I suppose? Not that I had a lot of choice, you understand."

Myrlin stepped back a little to allow me to swing down from the hammock. He was holding the gun in quite a relaxed way, not pointing it at me. Not that it would have mattered, of course, if he'd bent the barrel into a loop and thrown it away. There was no way I could imagine myself posing a threat to him. I couldn't remember having seen another humanoid on or off Asgard who could have gone two rounds with him without getting minced. I did a few token exercises to keep up appearances.

"How'd you find me?" I asked.

"Followed the tracks. I wasn't looking for you, but I knew you were ahead of me once I came to the place where you climbed out of the swamp."

"How come I was ahead of you?"

"I found out that you were on my trail when you reached the bottom of the downshaft and came within radio range," he said. "I knew the star-captain would carry on into the swamp if I laid the false trail. I doubled back, to await developments. I thought I might have to take care of the captain and her troopers."

"But not me?"

"What I overheard suggested that you weren't quite in accord with the star-captain. Of course, I don't know what they told you about me, so I can't calculate your attitude with any degree of certainty."

I decided that I'd duck that particular issue for the moment, and said: "Well, it seems that the swamp did your job for you.

There's only me and thee, now—unless you count Crucero and the guy guarding the trucks."

I knew before he replied that I was wrong. His pause was dripping with uncertainty. He must have been busy asking himself whether he could believe me. Being a trusting soul, he decided in favor.

"I didn't realize that you'd switched off," he said. "I thought you were just lying low, like me. It was on that assumption that I decided to approach you."

I realized then—perhaps belatedly—why he'd had me change frequency.

"How many are still alive?" I asked, feeling foolish.

"All of them," he said. "Whatever the screaming was about, it proved in the end to be harmless."

Praise the lord and pass the ammunition, I thought. *The wretched thing must have flowed right over them. Its juices couldn't pick a hole in their cold-suits.*

I made a mental note to write to the manufacturers, in case they wanted to put it in their advertising material for the benefit of future travelers in these happy climes.

"Well," I said, "if it's any comfort to you, knowing they were okay wouldn't have altered *my* behavior in the least. I suppose they know I'm still alive?"

"Yes."

"And they're not pleased?"

"The star-captain swears that she'll have you shot for desertion."

"Puts us into pretty much the same boat, doesn't it?"

"Perhaps," he answered cautiously.

I wondered whether it was a good time to ask why the star-captain was so very eager to see *him* dead, but decided to let the matter rest for a little while.

"We'd better get going," I said instead. "We haven't time to waste."

"I don't think they're likely to find us within the next few hours," he said. "They returned to the shaft to make new plans."

"Sod *them,*" I said scornfully. "I'm talking about following the tracks. I want to get to the city. A cold-suit will only keep you going for just so long—I've let enough time go by letting

Susarma Lear lead me on a wild goose chase through that god-damned swamp. Let's get down to business."

He made some inarticulate noise, which didn't sound like a veto, so I started packing up ready to move. He watched me, and didn't disturb me with questions. When I headed out into the open again he followed me meekly. That made me feel good. I couldn't exactly reckon on being in charge but, for the time being at least, I had things my own way.

Once we were walking, though, he returned to matters of mutual interest.

"While eavesdropping," he observed, "I heard passing mention of Amara Guur. You seem to think that he might be following you just as you are following me. I don't quite see how that could be—just as I'm not entirely sure how it is that you have managed to stick so close to *my* trail. Surely it's not so easy to track a man halfway across, and down inside, a world like Asgard?"

"I got hold of Saul Lyndrach's notebook," I told him. "I could read it—I think I'm the only man on Asgard who could."

"How did you get the notebook?"

"Jacinthe Siani—one of Guur's minions that you didn't eliminate—handed it over to me."

"In exchange for a translation?"

I was quick to deny that one. "No way," I said. "I knew those bastards had killed Saul. I wouldn't have given them the time of day. They'd just framed me into slavery, remember? No —they just handed the notebook to me. I won't say with no strings attached, because their purpose in doing it was to attach strings, but with no manifest demands. They planted some kind of bug in the book, of course, but I left that up on top. I think they also planted a bug—maybe more than one—on the star-captain. I don't know how it works, but I imagine they think it will help them find us even down here."

"You didn't tell the captain about the tag?" he inquired placidly. I noticed that he was using the correct colloquial term, where I'd carelessly used the wrong one. For a Salamandran android, if that's what he was, he was pretty well clued-up on idiomatically correct English.

"No I didn't," I said. "And you want to know why not, which is natural enough. It seemed like a good idea at the time, for several hazy reasons which don't seem quite so good now as they did then. Principally, I thought they might be biting off more than they could chew in coming into *my* territory. People like Guur and Heleb aren't down-level men—they're just petty gangsters. Guur's influence outside of the city is minimal, and his experience is nil. I wasn't worried much by the possibility of their getting on my tail. Anyhow, they weren't on *my* tail at all. It was the star-captain who got bugged—tagged, I mean—and I wasn't intending to stay with her quite as long as she had planned. I figured that she and Guur could fight it out between them. They seemed to deserve one another. Then again, while we were tagged, I was pretty sure that Guur and his heavies would keep a respectful distance, at least until we arrived some place worth being. I wasn't so sure they'd do that if we flushed the tags. Sometime, I'm going to have to get back to the surface, and I rather like the idea that I'll find my truck still there and my access to it unimpeded. If Guur's been greedy enough to follow us down here, hoping to dispose of us in the levels, there's a chance that I can get out. Whereas, if he were to decide that his best chance was to wait for me on level one in the hope of extracting by violent means from me what he failed to extract from Saul . . . I'd be in a bit of bother."

"And why don't those reasons seem so good now?"

I shrugged unnoticeably, inside my suit. "Now there's a possibility that Guur may be not too far away. I don't like the idea that he can creep up on me just the way you did, even if the possibility is remote. Also, though I have no particular liking for the star-captain, I can't help thinking that any man who'd let her go her merry way unaware of the fact that Amara Guur might know exactly where to find her just has to be a thoroughgoing bastard."

"You could have alerted her to the fact," he pointed out.

"Sure—but she wasn't planning on having me shot, then. I still had something to lose. Can you imagine her reaction if I'd turned around and told her that she was carrying a tag that she now couldn't get rid of, that I hadn't bothered to tell her about when she *could* have gotten rid of it? She's not exactly a mild-tempered person, you know."

"I know," he said softly.

We were still following the tracks in a landscape which was

by now depressingly familiar. The day before, it had been a wonderland of the unexpected; now it was as dull as ditch-water. It wasn't what I wanted, though I was sure that what I *did* want was somewhere to be found, at the far end of the rail-way. Until we got *there*, the time was just dead and empty as far as *my* main mission was concerned. I still wasn't too concerned about other people's projects, despite the fact that I was entangled with them. I guess I always was a touch egotistic. However, it didn't take too much time before striding along in silence began to get boring.

"Look," I said, struggling to keep up with him because his legs were longer than mine, "do you think you could possibly explain to me just what the hell is going on between you and the star-captain? Not that I want to get involved—I just want to know what it is that I've fallen into."

"How much do you know?" he asked.

"Hardly anything. It seemed to be a touchy subject. She says you're an android. She says you were made by the Salaman-drans, our enemies in a little interstellar skirmish which apparently ended with no more than a few billion casualties. She also says that you're a threat to the continued existence of the human race. I'm keeping an open mind about how much of that is true."

"The first two are true," he replied. "The last isn't. I'm no threat—but she does have a reason for thinking that I am, and I couldn't prove otherwise."

He stopped then, and I had to prompt him. "Try me," I said. "I might believe you. Anyone with half an eye could see that there's more in it for the captain than a sense of duty. She's practically rabid. Whatever you did to her, it was enough to make this *very* personal. I'm not about to take her side just because she's human."

There was a brief silence, and then he said: "All right. I'll tell it as I see it. You can decide later whether to believe it or not."

And he proceeded on exactly that basis.

26

Earth, it seemed, had always been winning the war. This small fact had apparently been much more obvious to the Salamandrans than to the humans, because only the Salamandrans knew how meager their resources were when it came to firepower. Earth's heavy metal technology was only a little more advanced than Salamandra's, in terms of the knowledge that was behind it, but knowledge doesn't turn into hardware automatically. Technology, as I'd earlier tried to explain to the starforce, is an art as well as a science. We humans, thinking always of technology in terms of machines, and mostly in terms of guns, had gained far more out by our knowledge of physics and chemistry than the enemy had. We had more guns, and a greater variety of guns.

The Salamandrans, though, were no primitives. Their knowledge was as wide and as sophisticated as ours—it was simply biased in a different way, oriented toward different practical skills. They were biotech fans, and much of their research and development was channeled into areas of expertise we had hardly touched. That had helped balance out the advantages in the war: in space, our ships and their firepower could always hand out a licking to theirs; but on the ground it was a different story. (When Myrlin explained all this, Serne's talk about sterile suits and germ warfare came to be seen in their proper perspective.) Their biotech capability had allowed the Salamandrans to destroy a lot of troops in the early part of the war, before Earth's high command caught on to the way things were and managed to put their men into the field with effective means of coping.

Seemingly, though, the Salamandrans had always known that their capabilities only allowed them to fight a holding action. They had known that Earth would find ways of canceling the biotech armory long before they could build any kind of defenses against the humans' heavy metal. They were sure right from the beginning that they were going to lose the war, and that the consequence of their losing it might be virtual genocide. They decided that their one chance of winning long-term domination over the region of space in dispute was to prepare for a second war, and lose the first one as cheaply as possible. Their idea was to buy time with the present fighting in order to launch a project which would ultimately turn the tables. By "ultimately," they meant after several generations—probably more than a thousand years. They were capable of taking the kind of long view that wouldn't make sense to most humans.

To the Salamandrans, warfare was primarily biological warfare. Their weapons were living creatures, ranging from artificial viruses to monsters engineered from vertebrate and invertebrate stock of many kinds. Against humans, the micro-organisms were the best weapons, largely because the difference of species meant that they didn't have to worry—as they would while fighting among themselves—about the weaponry rebounding on their own side. They tailored plagues to kill humans, but the rewards reaped by each new one grew less and less as Earth learned how to protect its armies and how to react to centers of infection among civilians. The human race lost a lot of its members, but the Salamandrans never succeeded in wiping out a human population, and on all worlds populated solely by humans their successes were extremely limited. They knew that if ever they were going to win a war against men, they would have to find a very clever means of opening up as many centers of infection as possible in such a short space of time that the fabric of human society, not just on one world but on many, would come apart at the seams before any response could be organized.

That wasn't an easy problem to solve, but they solved it. According to Myrlin, only two things went wrong. Firstly, they made some kind of cock-up in following a complicated recipe; and secondly, they ran out of time because the war reached Salamandra itself a couple of years too soon.

The plan was this. The Salamandrans set out to create human androids—androids so perfect in their duplication of humankind that they could cross-breed with normal individuals. Maybe "android" was the wrong term, except in a narrow technical sense; what they wanted was to make authentic people. These created humans were to be carriers of a deadly virus, but not in the straightforward sense that Typhoid Mary was a carrier. They would carry the virus locked into an inversion on one of their chromosomes, quite inert and unable to reproduce or do the slightest harm. The created men could mingle with other humans, and could settle down with them and have children. Half of their children would then become carriers, and half *their* children, and so on. All the while, nothing would show. While this was happening, the Salamandrans aimed to have surrendered, and to be patiently enduring the yoke of servitude, knowing that they had an ace up their sleeve. That ace, inevitably, was the trigger—an entirely harmless virus—that would unlock the inversion and release the genes programed to turn out deadly virions by the billion. By the time the trigger was to be released, enough humans on enough worlds would be genetically booby-trapped to ensure that as the trigger virus spread unnoticed it would touch off a series of epidemics sufficient to bring about the near-annihilation of the species.

Two things, as I said, went wrong. In preparation, it soon emerged that making the viruses was the easy part. Making the people was a problem of a very different kind. They had human prisoners, from whom they could obtain eggs and sperm, and the simplest plan would have been to booby-trap fertilized eggs and return the embryos to the wombs of female prisoners. The problem with that scheme, however, was that it left too much to chance. The carriers would be vulnerable for a long time— far *too* vulnerable. The possibility of losing the carriers while they were still infants was too great. The effort which the Salamandrans would have to put in to securing the children against the ravages of the war would be considerable.

So, the Salamandrans decided, they did not want to make booby-trapped babies. They wanted to make booby-trapped adults. What they wanted, in fact, was a regiment of human adult males of superior physique and intelligence (males, of course, on the supposition that the capacity to father children outweighs the capacity to mother them). They wanted individuals who would be quickly redistributed after the surrender, throughout human space, whose subversive careers could begin immediately. That, to the Salamandrans, looked a much better way to success than a regiment of babies which might be decimated, or even wiped out, before reaching reproductive age.

This was not too preposterous a thought for the Salamandrans to entertain, and was in keeping with their general lines of thought—which are, of course, quite alien to ours. They were already accustomed to sculpting the form and behavior of creatures native to their own and other worlds, and though they were cautious in tampering with the heredity of their own species they did that, too. The notion of producing adult individuals quickly, by rapidly accelerated growth, was not new to them. They had—not unnaturally—taken a keen interest in the biotech capabilities of other species, some of which had mastered tricks the Salamandrans had only dreamed about.

Apparently, the Salamandrans had invested heavily in alien biotechnics in order to get their project off the ground. Presumably they did not tell the sellers what the technics were to be used *for*, and presumably the sellers assumed that the purpose was quite innocent. Anyhow, with alien help the Salamandrans actually managed to get under way the scheme of growing adult humans (or reasonable facsimiles thereof), and of somehow programing the developing individuals in order to make them into people instead of human-shaped vegetables. My mind boggled at the thought of what this last part of the plan implied, but Myrlin assured me that hypnosuggestive techniques could equip brains with an adequate set of learning-programs and memory blocs in an astonishingly short period of time. It seems that we might overstress our uniqueness and our complexity, and that a man like me, for instance, didn't really need the experience of a lifetime to make me what I am. Everything that I am, it seems, could have been pumped in to me in a few months rather than all those years, if it had been boiled right down to the essentials. But I digress . . . suffice it to say that the plan was sound.

Except that the prototype turned out faulty. It wasn't a big fault, by any means (the pun is intended), and considering what they were attempting it must have been a very minor error against a background of dazzling success, but it was error enough.

When they took Myrlin out of his tank, he was just right. Physically perfect, apparently in his late twenties, believing himself to have been the son of a farmer on a colony world who'd been picked along with scores of others in the early part of the war and interned for the duration. His makers must have been cock-a-hoop . . . until they found out that he was still growing.

Somewhere, somehow, they'd overdone some magic ingredient, or failed to control some miraculous process. Myrlin was a working model, all right, but there was no way they could turn out a couple of hundred like him. If they were to proceed, they had to find out where they had made their mistake. A race of giants would be too conspicuous by far.

I've no doubt that they could have isolated the fault and worked the bug out of their system. Given three more years, Myrlin estimated, they might have managed to grow their small army of not-men whose unknowing destiny was to be the downfall of the human race. They didn't get their three years. They didn't even get one. The juggernaut of human heavy metal mowed down the Salamandran legions, and the home-world was under siege even before the second prototype enjoyed his strange birth. Plans were hurriedly made to try to carry on in secret—to preserve one tiny base of operations which could do its deadly work while the rest of Salamandra kept the invaders looking another way—but even that was not to be. A platoon of starship troopers mopping up after the battle of Salamandra's skies practically fell on top of the crucial installation, and stormed it without the least suspicion of what it might be. It had guards and a perimeter fence built to keep the locals at bay—those two things were enough to make it a target for Susarma Lear's commandos.

The star-captain had found Myrlin imprisoned in a steel cage somewhere in the base. Not unnaturally, she had let him out. The story he told was convincing enough—after all, *he* knew no better—and there was only one of him. At an individual level, being well over seven feet tall may be unusual, but it isn't enough to make people leap to the conclusion that you're an alien monster.

After being let out, Myrlin had simply stayed around. The Salamandrans, having lost the fight for the base, had set out to destroy all evidence of what they'd done, and had almost succeeded before the star-captain had stopped them. She'd called in Military Intelligence as a result of the attempt, and Myrlin had been co-opted to help them find out what the mystery was. When he found out—a little ahead of M.I., thanks to the knowledge he already had and which began to make sense to him before it began to make sense to *them*—he had tried to finish the job his makers had started. He didn't want the truth about himself to be known, once he realized what the outcome of the revelation might be. All that would be *necessary*, of course, would be for him to be sterilized, but even a few days' acquaintance with star-captains and the officers of Military Intelligence had made him conscious of the fact that they wouldn't settle for that. In their eyes, he wasn't human. They'd have disposed of him without the ghost of a moral qualm.

He hadn't succeeded, though, in completing the cover-up. What made things worse—if there was any way they *could* be worse—was the fact that his attempt was discovered. Figuring that any slim chance he'd had of staying alive was blown, he'd made his exit from the scene of the crime as quickly as possible. With Susarma Lear and her battle-weary platoon in pursuit, he'd made his way across the war-torn face of Salamandra, staying clear of trouble until he managed to con his way onto a shuttle that took him into orbit. Had the military been able to coordinate their operations better, he wouldn't have stood a dog's chance, but in the aftermath of a horribly brutal war, nothing runs with clinical efficiency. He made it to an operational star-station, and there he brought off one of the most glamorous and difficult of all crimes. He stole a starship.

Myrlin, in his narrative, skipped over most of the details. He talked about things I knew to be bordering on the impossible in a matter-of-fact tone that made them seem almost commonplace. It was beyond the capacity of my imagination to picture the circumstances as they must have been on the surface of Salamandra—a surface torn apart by firepower, where some considerable fraction of the population must have been wiped out. It must have been a very special kind of hell. Yet this man —this being—who was, in effect, newborn had made his way there, unscathed, and had managed to escape from it despite the fact that there was absolutely no one to whom he could turn for help.

"All I can say," I said, when he finished his story, "is that they must have done a magnificent job of filling your head."

"Yes," he agreed. "I think they must."

27

"So," I said, "you're no threat."

"I wasn't planning on having children," he said. "And even if I had a dozen, who each had a dozen of their own . . . the gun no longer has a trigger. Humanity has nothing to fear."

"Why didn't they just let you go? They must realize that."

"It's not so simple," he replied. "Not from their point of view. They can't look inside my head. They don't know who or what I am, here inside, and they'd never be willing to trust me. From their viewpoint, I'm something that looks human but is really Salamandran. They think of me as some kind of double agent—an infiltrator and a subversive. For all they know, I might be fully aware of my Salamandran origin, loyal to the anti-human cause. I'm safer dead, and they want me dead. They'd never take the chance of letting me live an ordinary life. I can see their point. I can appreciate the deep hatred they have of all things Salamandran. They've just come through a bitter and vicious war the like of which human beings have never known before."

I'd have liked to be able to see his face, to read its expressions, but all I had was a disembodied voice, calm and flat, made calmer and flatter by the radio link itself.

"Besides," he said, "for the captain, it's personal. She was the one who let me out. She was in technical command of the base where I tried to destroy material relevant to the war effort, and from which I made my escape. From her viewpoint, those were mistakes, and though every one is understandable in the abstract, they're not mistakes for which she can readily forgive herself."

"She's not the forgiving type," I agreed. "I daresay she'd be even tougher with herself than with her men. It's a crazy story all around, but when crazy people are in crazy circumstances, I guess that's the kind of story which fits."

"You believe me, then?"

"Sure," I said. "Why not?"

We were still walking the line, and there was still nothing to see. I knew that Asgard was a big place, and that one couldn't rely on stumbling upon a city every time one went for a little stroll, but I was beginning to get impatient.

"Pity they didn't manage to keep the train running, as long as they were feeding power in anyway," I observed.

"What makes you think there's power here?" asked Myrlin. "This ecology's run wild. It could be sustained by purely cyclic processes."

"Life-systems need energy inputs," I told him. "They can't feed off themselves indefinitely. This one may have degenerated in the sense that it's lost its old functional organization, but it would have decayed into ooze long ago without some input—probably heat diffusing outwards from lower levels. Maybe only a trickle, but it has to be there to keep entropy at bay. They didn't put that in your head, then?"

"No," he replied, "they didn't put that in my head. They gave me a biography, three languages, and a good stock of knowledge, but mostly they stuck to basics. I suppose I'm more intelligent than most, and I've got a fair range of skills, but the idea was to turn out a human being, not a superman."

"Where do you think they got it? The biography—the stocks of common knowledge that a human might have. It's not something that'd be easy to put together piece by piece."

He sighed audibly. "I expect that the biography was mostly borrowed," he said. "Maybe they didn't even change the name. I changed it, mind—Myrlin isn't what *they* gave me. I daresay that everything they put into me had to be leached out of real people at one time or another, one way or another. There's nothing supernatural about it, though—it wasn't some kind of mechanical telepathy, or some soul-stealing process that sucked the spirit out of one man and pumped it into me. I got my mind the way you got yours—the input came into my senses, albeit in an unorthodox fashion."

"There are still a few little gaps," I said. "I guess most of them aren't really in your province. But one that is—why Asgard? Why come here, with a whole galaxy to choose from?"

"That's simple enough," he said. "There's a peculiar sense in which I originated here. I said that the Salamandrans bought alien help. I'm not altogether sure who from, but I saw documents with a symbol shaped like *this*"—he drew a picture in the empty air with the forefinger of his right gauntlet—"and references to Asgard. I figured that it might be a good idea to know a little bit more about my background. I didn't realize then, of course, that the technics which the Salamandrans bought were the legacy of a race that's been a long time dead—or, at least, out of sight for millions of years."

I'd already stopped dead in astonishment.

"Jesus Christ!" I said. "You mean that someone's got something *that* rich out of the junk men like me have been dragging back from the levels?"

"It would seem so."

"They kept bloody quiet about it."

"They would," said Myrlin, "wouldn't they?"

He was *so* right. Indeed, he might be righter than he knew. I was willing to take oath that Aleksandr Sovorov knew nothing about achievements of that level, of that kind. But then, the moral of Myrlin's story, if it had a moral at all, was surely the fact that we sometimes miss realizing how limited our imaginative vision really is when it comes to the artistry of technology. Alex was on the trail of bigger and better mousetraps, clad in chromium-plated steel. Humans don't think biotech the way that, for instance, the Tetrax do.

"What would you have done if that kind of technology had been in constant operation here?" I asked. "Or was it mere vulgar curiosity about your family tree?"

"I don't know," he said. "Maybe I'd have commissioned the building of an appropriate bride. Isn't that what Frankenstein's monster asked for?"

"You've read *Frankenstein?*"

"No, but I remember hearing the story. Remember, I guess, in quotation marks."

The exchange was slightly acid, and I didn't want that. Far be it from me to make a big thing out of his ignoble origins. I didn't continue to insult him by asking whether he'd want his bride made up with or without genetic booby-traps with long time fuses.

"So," I said, "what now?"

"Now," he replied, in measured tones, "I'm with you. Looking for a way to the center. For no better reason than you have, I suppose. It's a chance to lose the people who want to kill me, and it seems to me that if you're running away, you might as well have somewhere to aim for. Not so?"

It seemed to me that he was implying that *I* was running away, too—and not just from blonde star-captains who had threatened to shoot me for desertion. I let it pass. If he thought he was qualified as a psychoanalyst on the strength of a mere few months of being human, let him. *I* didn't have to take any notice.

"I don't know if you've already observed this," he said, "but the horizon has grown noticeably brighter these last few minutes. I think that your city is not very far away—and I think that it has not quite succumbed to the kind of chaos we see around us now."

I *hadn't* observed it, and I cursed myself for getting lost in a maze of thoughts which had served to distract me from the really important issue at stake. At the same time, though, I offered silent thanks for the answer to my prayer. Here, it seemed, was a chance to take the next step in the long and arduous journey to the heart of the mystery that was Asgard.

28

I was hoping for something unexpected—something that would really bend my mind. I knew that we weren't far below surface, but still I was hoping to meet the men who built Asgard. If that turned out not to be, there were a thousand unforeseen alternatives I would have settled for quite happily.

As always happens in these cases, though, I got only the least part of my wish. What we found in the city was certainly unexpected.

The city was decaying, like everything else on this level. It had been decaying, slowly, for a very long time. Walls were crumbling, doorways yawned, the streets were filthy with slime and debris. The one thing untouched by the heavy hand of time was the system of city lights—no frail bioluminescence had ever held domain over this place; it was illuminated by white light from a million incandescent bulbs, each one the size of a man's head. There was not a single dead bulb: the repair system which kept the lights in good order was obviously functional.

What the lights displayed to us, though, was strange to behold in quite a different way. There was no need for us to search for the inhabitants of the city, for they came to us, attracted like night-flying insects to a flame. The metaphor is more appropriate than perhaps it seems, for though they were attracted there was nothing in their eyes to suggest that they were moved by any active curiosity; instead, their vacant expressions suggested that they were *drawn* by some inner impulse which they could not or did not care to suppress.

They were humanoid, but on a scale I had not seen among all the starfaring races whose members congregated on Asgard. Those fully grown had the height of a human child of eleven or twelve Earthly years, but not the build. They were thin and bony, and their heads were small and elongated. Their skin was silver-grey and wrinkled, so that even the small children barely able to walk had faces that seemed irredeemably ancient. They were clothed, but most wore only filthy loincloths, and even the most extravagantly dressed had only knee-length trousers and little jerkins that were tattered and threadbare.

As the crowd assembled—not *around* us, but to either side of us—I noted that not a single one was carrying anything. No tools, no weapons. There was no sign that any of them had been *doing* anything that our arrival had interrupted, except for some of the children, who abandoned games played with pebbles in order to stare at us.

Not one of them made any kind of approach toward us. None tried to get in our way. They just watched us as we walked through the streets, and most—not all—then followed us, so that the retinue trailing behind us grew steadily larger.

"If these are the descendants of the men who built Asgard," I muttered, "then I'm the bastard son of a toothless Tetron."

"They're degenerate," observed Myrlin. "They could be descended from *anyone*. You can't judge what they once were from what they are now."

"The inherited decadence of dependence on machines?" I countered. "It's a myth. The idea that evolution goes into reverse gear when natural selection eases up is based on a fallacy.

The removal of selective pressure may stop the replacement of mediocre genes by better ones, but it can't promote the replacement of adequate ones by poorer ones. Relative advantage still works the same way—deleterious mutations still tend to be selected out.

"No—if the members of this race were ever very much taller than they are now, the loss is probably due to malnutrition or psychosocial dwarfism, not to any genetic drift. If their apparent stupidity is real, it's culturally transmitted. Learned helplessness. Anyhow, there *is* selective pressure. There has to be. Out beyond the city limits, there are some very nasty critters. They'd be here, making an easy meal out of our crazy friends if they always behaved like this. They're reacting this way to *us* because they have no reason to fear us. . . . In fact, more than that, because they *are* reacting, not just ignoring us. That implies. . . ."

"That giants in cold-suits are a familiar sight hereabouts," Myrlin finished for me. He tried to make it sound unlikely.

"Not cold-suits," I answered. "But maybe *sterile* suits. Nobody can tell me that those city lights kept shining while the countryside went to hell on the basis of their own automatic repair systems. Someone comes here. Someone from down below. They don't use the shaft *we* used. Ergo they use another."

"Wishful thinking," said Myrlin.

He was right, of course. My thinking was just about as wishful as thinking can be. But that didn't affect the underlying logic.

I stopped, and turned around to face the crowd that was following us. There must have been four hundred and more by now, mostly adults. A lot of the ones who had dropped out, or never fallen into step, were children.

When I stopped, they stopped. Myrlin had to come back a couple of strides.

"What is it?" he asked.

"Wishful thinking," I said. "*Look* at them, damn it! Why are they following us? There has to be a reason. It's not childlike stupidity mingled with all-round curiosity. It's a *response* that's somehow imprinted into them, and it has to have some kind of rationale. You tell me—what is it?"

He looked down at them from his lofty station. "It's weird," he agreed. "But don't ask me. I'm only a poor android, remember."

I looked at the crowd searchingly, wondering if that might be what *they* were, if the technics that helped create Myrlin had really once been commonplace among the inhabitants of Asgard. I discarded the hypothesis. Right or wrong, it didn't help to explain a single thing.

"If they're following us," I said, "it's because they expect some kind of payoff. A handout."

"Maybe they assume we're gods," ventured Myrlin. "Perhaps they want miracles—or simply a kind word and a gesture of approval."

I didn't bother to reply to that one. I just scanned the sea of wrinkled faces, searching for one that showed signs of inspiration. I wanted some kind of lead. Myrlin turned again, ready to start walking, but when I didn't move he stopped again.

No one was in any hurry, but in the end the tension was too much for them. One of their number was pushed forward until he was so exposed he had no alternative but to take responsibility. He came forward, until he was standing a couple of meters away, then he squinted up into Myrlin's face (is there anywhere in the universe where people don't correlate size with authority?) and began talking.

Not unnaturally, it wasn't pangalactic *parole* he was spouting.

I waved my arms to signify that I wasn't getting it, tapped my helmet in an attempt to let him know that I couldn't hear, then tapped the palm of one hand with the forefinger of the other to suggest that he try sign language. He wasn't very quick on the uptake, and I had to carry on the pantomime. I pointed in four different directions, and tried to indicate that I didn't know which way to go. I mimed walking and tried to communicate to him the fact that I wanted him to guide me. I couldn't tell him where to, because I didn't know—I was hoping he had one or two ideas of his own on that subject. For a while, it seemed like a vain hope. I might have been doing a mating dance or dancing a jig, so far as he was concerned.

Somewhere in the crowd, though, the penny dropped. Some local genius finally figured out that we were all standing around because nobody knew where we ought to be going, and figured that it was up to him to think of a destination. He thrust his way forward, babbled at the spokesman for a few moments, caught himself an argument, won it, and eventually moved on ahead of us. He looked back at us expectantly.

I gave him a star-force salute and said, "Take me to your leader."

Then the procession started up again.

We continued in the direction we had been following before the halt, and deviated neither to right nor left for such a long time that I began to wonder whether the man who led us was not actually guiding us but simply going first along the path which he believed us to have chosen.

In our wake, the crowd grew, but slowly. More dropped out as we took them, perhaps, farther than they cared to go, and the total number never exceeded the thousand mark. The city had apparently been built to house a great many more people than were now living in it, but it was nevertheless reasonably populous, in my judgment. This was no mere family group, however extended their concept of the family might be.

At last, though, we turned aside, and found ourselves quickly drawn into a new area of the city, where the dilapidated dwellings gave way to larger buildings, presumably public buildings of various kinds. Most of these had suffered more from the ravages of time than the simpler units, and more than half of them were reduced to rubble or to gaunt skeletons of stony pillars and wrecked arches. Spears of shadow criss-crossed the cracked and much-begrimed pavements on which we walked, especially when we crossed open plazas where the lighting was less regular.

My heartbeat sped up when I saw the place to which our guide had brought us. It was a hemispherical dome, brilliantly lighted from within so that light beams radiated like spines from its many rounded windows. Alone among all the buildings it seemed untouched by decay. It did not belong.

Our guide took us right to the door—a great circular portal that looked like the airlock on a giant starfreighter. There he stood aside and beckoned us nearer, indicating by signs fully as expressive as my own that we should go on without him.

We would have, too, were it not for the fact that the door

was tightly sealed, and we had not the slightest idea how it might be opened. There was some kind of panel beside the door, set in the curved surface of the dome, but that was shielded by a plate of transparent plastic that did not yield to the gentle pushing and prising of our fingers.

The crowd was still there, still waiting.

"I'm beginning to feel like a bit of a fool," I confessed to Myrlin, after several minutes of probing and prodding in the region of the door and its presumed locking mechanism.

Myrlin was already unbuckling his cutting apparatus. I watched him dubiously, not sure that it was the right thing to do, but unable to think of any alternative.

I took out a knife, and used the blade to try to lever off the plate covering the panel which presumably controlled the door. I couldn't get it loose.

"It's not just a dust cover," opined Myrlin. "It's some kind of seal. Let me take it."

I moved out of his way, and he activated the beam of the cutter. I glanced around to see if the crowd was reacting at all, but they simply watched us with saintly patience.

Myrlin cut the center out of the plate in a matter of seconds. The plastic shriveled at the first breath of the beam. He switched off and knocked it out of the way. Then he began pressing the large button in the middle of the panel beneath.

Nothing happened. When he stood aside to let me try, I drew his attention to a vertical slit left of center.

"That," I said, "looks for all the world like a keyhole."

"Wary of interference, aren't they?" he replied.

"What now?" I asked.

I was thinking along the lines of taking stock of our situation, looking around for a while, talking things over and that kind of thing. Myrlin, however, was plainly a man of action—or perhaps he simply reacted badly to frustration. He simply switched the cutter beam back on, increased the power to maximum, and thrust the head of the damned thing into the panel box. The plastic of the buttons began to sizzle and the metal of the console flared as it melted.

"Hey!" I said. "You'd better be. . . ."

I was interrupted by the fact that all the lights in the dome—in fact, all the lights in the city—suddenly went out.

The patient crowd finally lost patience. They *ran*—scuttled for cover like panicked rabbits.

When the lights came back on again, after an interval of maybe half a minute, we were alone.

"I think you blew the circuit," I said to Myrlin.

"It repaired itself," he pointed out.

There was something different about the quality of the light, but it took me a moment or two to work out just what it was. It was no longer entirely white, and it was no longer as steady as it had been. The city lights were the same, but inside the dome something had changed. There was nothing to be seen through the windows at ground level but a long, featureless corridor that apparently went all around the dome. That was still lit. Higher up, though, there were intermittent flashes of red modifying the beams of white.

I marveled at the long arm of coincidence. A thousand light-years from Earth, deep inside a gigantic artificial world, they used flashing red lights as alarm signals. I was still thinking to myself that the galaxy was quite a homely place after all when the door began to open. The hinge was at the top, and it swung outward to extend a vast curved shadow.

We moved, reflexively, into the shadow, ready to meet whatever came out of the door. The sudden blaze of light took us by surprise, and dazzled me so completely that I couldn't see a thing. I heard Myrlin cry out in pained surprise, and then felt a horrid sensation as though acid was being poured into my brain.

I *screamed*.

Maybe Myrlin did too, but I was in no fit condition to hear him. There was a moment when I thought my soul was being torn apart, and then consciousness deserted me for what seemed to be a long, long time.

Crazy as it may seem, I woke up feeling good. I had long regarded it as an inevitable aspect of the human condition that no one, whatever the circumstances, *ever* wakes up feeling good, but this was an exceptional awakening in more ways than one. I felt fresh, lightheaded and euphoric.

I was lying on my side, on hard ground, with no pillow for my head, but I wasn't stiff or uncomfortable—which suggested that I hadn't been there long. When I opened my eyes I seemed to be in bright daylight, and there was fresh green grass on the ground. It felt good, brushing my cheek, and it smelled good too. When I tried to move, I felt an eccentric rush of nostalgia that took me right back to early days in the belt. The gravity couldn't have been any more than a quarter Earth normal.

I could have stayed there enjoying myself for quite a while, if I'd managed to keep disturbing thoughts at bay. Maybe I should have. It was a long time since I'd felt that good, and once I began to think about how wrong it all was I cast aside the possibility of feeling so good again for a long time.

The first thing that jarred my sense of well-being was the realization that light gravity and green grass don't go together. The next thing I managed to recall was that I was neither in the belt nor on Earth, but on a crazy world named Asgard. Then it all came back, and I felt a moment of stark terror as I became aware that I could feel, smell and hear the grass and things moving in it—which meant, of course, that something very important to me was missing: the helmet of my cold-suit. I searched quickly back through the vestiges of my memory, trying to figure out which was the last thing that had happened to me. It took some figuring—I seemed to be quite disconnected from the past—and when I did settle upon the correct image it seemed unusually remote, like something that had happened a long time ago, far away from wherever I was now.

That last image, of course, was the memory of that big airlock door swinging open, of Myrlin and me stepping into its shadow, and of being hit by a mindscrambler—something very much akin to the thing the peace officers carry in Skychain City. As I pieced things together again, I realized that there was an awful lot to be worried about. A little mild panic would not have been out of order. But the one realization that loomed larger than all the rest, bringing with it a ludicrous sensation of utter triumph and exultation, was the significance of the low gravity.

The bottom of Saul Lyndrach's dropshaft had been so close to the surface of Asgard that the loss in weight had been unnoticeable. I had been a long, long way from the center, no matter how important the discovery of all those new levels might be. Wherever I was now, though, had to be a *lot* deeper. If I was still on Asgard (and I could hardly doubt that) then I must be closer to the Center than to the surface.

Hence exultation: I was *here*; I had *arrived*.

But where was *here*?

I looked quickly around. I was not, of course, under a daylit sky; the ceiling was less than half a kilometer above my head. It was glossy white set with twisting ribbons of light that would have been pretty to look at if they hadn't been so dazzling. The uneven grass-covered ground stretched away in front of me, broken up by clumps of trees and undulating mounds of flowering plants. I could hear sounds that seemed to be insect wings, but couldn't catch more than a glimpse of anything flying.

When I turned around to see whether it was the same behind me, I got a shock. Thirty meters away there was a wall, and no ordinary wall. It stretched from the ground all the way up to the ceiling, white and featureless. It ran away to the left and the right as far as I could see, curving very gently. The curve looked to me like the arc of a circle, though I couldn't be sure whether that impression was trustworthy. For all I knew, it might be a weird optical illusion, but if it wasn't, there was every possibility that I was in some kind of enclosure, maybe a few kilometers in diameter.

The conclusion I jumped to was that I'd been deposited in some kind of landscaped cage. It wasn't a nice conclusion.

I was still wearing my cold-suit, all except the helmet, of which there was no sign. The backpack was still there, and the tools I'd been carrying were still at my waist, buckled in their normal positions. Only one thing was gone—the knife with which I'd tried to open the control-panel beside the big round door. That had still been in my hand when the mindscrambler hit me. I had no flame pistol, of course—Myrlin had never offered to return it to me.

I looked around for Myrlin, but there was no sign of him.

What a way to open a dialogue between worlds, I thought. *You'd think the lousy bastards would be glad we'd found them, after all this time.*

There didn't seem to be any point in staying where I was, so I began walking. I followed the line of the wall, figuring that somewhere along its length there was bound to be a door. My recent experiences with doors had been a trifle disappointing, but there seemed to be very little alternative to plugging on and hoping my luck would change.

I thought over my predicament while I walked. I figured that the suit's internal hook-ups were probably okay—I certainly couldn't feel anything wrong—and that I presumably wouldn't have to worry about foraging for roots and berries for a while. I couldn't feel any symptoms which implied that the metabolic control system was out of kilter, so the suit ought to maintain me for a good many days yet. How many, I wasn't sure—I had no idea how long I'd been unconscious. There was no reason to think that it might have been days rather than hours (my chronometer, of course, was in my helmet where I could normally see it) but that feeling of remoteness from my last conscious moments persisted.

The air I was breathing seemed perfectly all right, better than the substandard stuff the Tetrax used to supply the needs of their manifold guests in the Skychain City dome. In a way, that was reassuring, as I didn't much want to collapse from hyperoxygenation or carbon monoxide poisoning or whatever, but there was also a sense in which it was disquieting. It suggested *planning* on the part of whoever had put me here, and might just imply that they had set things up for a long stay. I didn't really want to spend the rest of my life here.

On the other hand, if I didn't find my helmet, I wasn't likely to have much choice. Whatever else was between me and the surface, there were certainly several levels where the atmosphere was mostly snow.

It didn't take me long to get used to the light gravity. It was a long time since I'd been in the belt, but when you've spent more than fifteen of your most impressionable years in conditions where gravity varying between zero and Earth-normal is part and parcel of everyday life, you learn adjustment skills that you never lose. I made mistakes, of course—overstriding and over-balancing frequently—but mistakes aren't penalized heavily in quarter-gravity, and the main thing was that I *felt* okay. I even took a couple of big jumps in case I could get up high enough to see over the trees that were blocking my view, but all I got was a different angle on the greenery.

I suppose I was careless—I wasn't expecting trouble, in spite of all I'd been through, though if my natural pessimism had been at full strength I would have *known* that things weren't going to stay simple. Anyhow, I was breezing along looking at the wall and wondering about what was on the other side of it, when I walked straight into the worst situation that I could have found.

Obviously they'd seen me coming. When they stepped out of hiding they were covering every direction I might run, and they had their guns already drawn.

The one in front of me had a needle gun pointed at my midriff in the most insultingly casual fashion. All vormyr look alike to me, but I could safely have bet my soul that I could guess his name in one.

"Hello, Mr. Rousseau," he said. "I knew we'd meet again, someday."

I'd stopped dead, of course. I spread my hands wide to indicate that I had no weapon.

"Regrettably," I said, "it's Trooper Rousseau of the Earth Star-force. If you were to use that gun it would constitute an act of war against the human race."

There were two other faces I knew, apart from Amara Guur's. One was Jacinthe Siani, another was the Spirellan, Heleb. There were two more vormyr. Everybody was armed—even Jacinthe. It was she who approached me and began to strip off my belt and backpack. Apparently they didn't want me to improvise anything that could be used to hurt them. I could tell by the way she fumbled that the gravity was affecting her far more than me.

"Where are the others?" asked Guur. I think he was smiling, but I'm not sure.

"I don't know," I told him. "I woke up alone. Can't you track down the star-captain with your electronic bloodhound?"

There isn't any way to say "bloodhound" in *parole*, so he lost the meat of the metaphor, but he chortled anyway—a blood-curdling sight.

"You really fell for that?" he asked. "We did sprinkle a few little toys in the captain's lovely blonde hair, but that was merely a decoy. The *real* tag is inside your bootheel. You've been leaving electronic footprints ever since you left the dome. Saul Lyndrach took your truck and cold-suit—we knew that you'd have to order a replacement. We have . . . influence . . . with the suppliers."

My heart sank. I didn't like to be played for a fool. I didn't like to be forced to recognize that I *could* be played for a fool. And so easily, too.

"On the other hand," Guur went on, "if you didn't bother to get rid of the other transmitters, perhaps we *can* find the star-captain. I'd rather like to have the advantage, if and when we meet."

I cursed myself again, and made a mental note to censor any future comments I might feel inspired to make.

Heleb had moved to Guur's side, though the other two vormyr hovered behind me still.

"Kill him," suggested the Spirellan.

"No!" said Guur. He looked at his followers one by one. "No one harms him—that must be understood." Then he turned to me, and said: "I play the game honorably, do I not?"

"Like hell," I said. "You know where we are, and you know full well that you can't shoot your way out. The six of us don't have a single helmet between us. We're stuck in some tiny little ecobubble several thousand kilometers below the surface of Asgard. You're no better off than I am despite the needlers and the crash-guns. You figure that you might need me, if ever any of us are going to find out why we're here and what prospects there are of getting out."

"It would be as well if you avoided an inflated opinion of your usefulness," observed Jacinthe Siani. "I can hardly imagine that *your* brain will add significantly to our resources." She glanced at Amara Guur, but he made no comment.

I shrugged. "Okay," I said, trying to inject some sarcasm into a dialogue that really wasn't adapted to it. "I'm entirely at your disposal. I'll try not to be too much of a nuisance."

Guur gestured with the needler. "You may as well keep

going, Trooper Rousseau. I assume there is nothing in the direction from which you've come. We may as well try the other. Jacinthe—try to get a reading on those microtransmitters the star-captain may still be carrying. Heleb—cover the right flank."

We all did as we were told. For the time being, Amara Guur was in sole charge of our collective destiny.

We hadn't gone far before Jacinthe Siani announced that she was getting a reading on the tag that had been planted on Susarma Lear. She was using some kind of hand-held receiver which gave her direction only, but when she pointed it was obvious that the star-captain and her comrades weren't so very far away. Assuming the wall to be following the arc of a circle, the line the Kythnan woman described was a chord, probably no more than seven or eight hundred meters long.

We stopped.

"Are they coming toward us, or moving away?" asked Guur.

Jacinthe Siani shook her head. Guur took the receiver from her, and watched it for a few moments. "I think they're following the wall," he said, his voice scratchy and guttural. After a few more moments passed, he added: "This way." Then he switched out of *parole* and into what was presumably his own language. He gave orders rapidly.

The two other vormyr faded back into the bushes. Jacinthe Siani handed over her weapon to Guur, and moved off in the other direction, toward the star-captain.

Guur gestured to me, and said: "Sit."

I sat down. Heleb glowered at me, and then took up a position a little forward of me, with his back to us. Guur came close to me, and squatted on his haunches a meter or so away, for all the world like a snake ready to strike.

"Why are we here, Mr. Rousseau?" he asked quietly.

"So now you want a discussion on philosophy?" I parried. The expression on his face changed my mind about merry banter. The way he looked, I knew that I could be dead at any minute. He would casually cut me up without a moment's thought, if the impulse came over him.

"I will tell you what I know," he said. "We were taken by some kind of machine, while we still followed the rails. There was bright light, then some kind of confusion-device. I am conscious of nothing more, but I know that happened some twelve days ago."

"*Twelve days!*"

He ignored the interruption. "I assume that we have been subjected to a very thorough examination. I think the reason for putting us in this cage must be to continue with that examination. We are being watched, Mr. Rousseau. Now—I know that you saw more than we did. Do you know anything else?"

"You're sure about the twelve days?"

"There are internal physiological cycles which allow time to be measured," was his only reply.

I shook my head. "I can't add anything. I got to the city at the far end of the track. There were humanoids there, but they were no more intelligent than young children. Someone from down below obviously sees to it that basic supplies are maintained. Light, of course—I suspect food, too. When we started interfering with the systems, we were zapped almost immediately. Light to dazzle us, then the mindscrambler. I guess you're right—they want to know about us. We're trapped on a microscope slide, and they're watching our every move. They're not going to get a very favorable impression of us, are they?"

"Why do you say that?"

"I thought the shooting war was about to break out?"

Guur grunted. "Jacinthe has gone to negotiate a cease-fire with the star-captain. She and I have no quarrel."

I decided to make no comment on that. "What about Myrlin?" I said. "Susarma Lear isn't going to stop shooting at him —and neither, unless I'm much mistaken, is your loyal henchman the Spirellan."

Guur was silent for a moment, and then said: "When you assume that they will think badly of us if they see us fight, you take it for granted that they are fruit-eaters, like the Tetrax."

I gathered that he didn't think too much of the Tetrax.

"Not necessarily," I said. "But this may be the first time they've realized that there are people wandering around on the skin of their big steel onion. They might not even have known that there was anyone else in the universe except themselves. If you were in that position, and you found people wandering around up there, what kind of people would *you* like them to be?"

He replied with a Vormyran word. When I waited, he said: "It means 'things edible,' in a special sense. Prey."

"You can't treat people as prey," I told him.

His face changed. I hadn't thought it could become more threatening, but I was wrong.

"The ethics of the herd," he said. "Who says so, save for fruit-eaters? There are two kinds of creatures, my friend—those whose way it is to eat, and those whose way it is to feed on grass and fruit and to be eaten. The law demands loyalty to the tribe, respect for fellow predators, and ruthless exploitation of the other kind. That is how *real* people live. *That* is civilization."

One tends to assume that gangsters are inarticulate. I had always resented the fact that the Tetrax consider human beings to be barbaric, but in the case of the vormyr I had thought they were simply recognizing the obvious. Thinking about it, though, I shouldn't have been surprised to find that the vormyr had their own views.

"You can't discriminate between intelligent humanoids on the basis of what they eat," I told him. "The distinction between creatures that think and creatures that don't must have priority over the distinction between carnivores and herbivores." *Myself*, I added silently, *I'm an omnivore and proud of it.*

He didn't answer me, save with what I took to be a contemptuous glare. He didn't have to put the answer into words. Whose judgment of priorities were we taking? The judgment of a lousy bunch of fruit-eaters? For the vormyr, obviously, the priority was the other way around. When you met a stranger on Vor, or whatever they called their homeworld, you didn't ask whether he was a fellow sentient or not—you asked whether or not he was fit to be eaten. They'd carried the same protocol into space. No wonder they weren't very popular. No wonder they set up their own criminal subculture in defiance of the law framed by the Tetrax and their allies.

I recalled that Sleaths were vegetarian. It no longer seemed in the least surprising that they'd murdered a man just to put a frame on me. To Guur and his kind it wasn't murder. Sleaths and the like were due not an atom of moral consideration—they were simply there to be used. I began to realize how ambiguous my own situation was. It wasn't a comfortable thought.

"You think the men who built Asgard are carnivores?" I asked.

He had looked away, watching Heleb for some sign that Jacinthe Siani might be returning. Now he looked back at me, his red eyes gleaming in a fashion that seemed to me diabolical.

"No," he answered. "They are leaf-eaters."

"In the levels," I said, "there's plenty of evidence that they kept livestock. Sure, they had extensive agricultural projects, but they ate meat."

"In their thoughts," he said, "they are leaf-eaters."

"How do you figure that?"

"Armor," he said. "Armor is the investment of leaf-eaters. The predator is sleek and moves fast. None but those who feed on seed and branch would armor a world and hide in its bowels. As for their prey—though that is too dignified a word—they neither hunt it nor eat it raw. If they could, they would grow it entirely in machines, as the Tetrax do. Their habits are unclean and vile. The universe, it seems, is full of herds, but the law bids predators be prudent. The predator is clever, the predator deceives. The *future* is ours. The ethics of the herd will preserve the herd, until the day of the hunter comes. Can you doubt it?"

I could doubt it all right, but that wasn't the point that interested me for the moment. I could see where I fit into the vormyran scheme of things now. Omnivore I might be, but in his book I was a herbivore in spirit.

"As I said," I murmured, "they're not going to get a very good impression of us, are they?" Even as I said it, I remembered *his* words. *The predator is clever; the predator deceives.*

"The star-captain won't fall for it," I told him. "There's a lot of the predator about her, too."

He looked steadily into my face, and said: "Your kind is irredeemably confused. You try to follow the law *and* the ethics of the herd, at one and the same time. You seek a balance which cannot exist. If ever you are to become whole, you must go one way or the other. You must choose the herd or the tribe. Balidar chose the tribe. I think your star-captain is the same. But you . . . I think you are a Tetron, at heart. Perhaps as little as a Sleath."

I didn't feel much like a Tetron or a Sleath, but I wasn't entirely sure that I ought to feel insulted. I didn't feel like a vormyran either. While I hovered in search of a coherent reaction, I realized that I was proving his point by default. I *was* confused, between his kind of 'law' and the so-called ethics of the herd. I salved my conscience by wondering whether that confusion was such a bad thing. Then I wondered if that Tetron theory of history with the idiotic name had any way of figuring in the vormyran concept of destiny. Probably not. And yet, each in their way aimed at the eventual dominance of some kind of slave system.

Any *decent* man, I decided, had every right to be confused. *Omnivores of the universe, unite!* I thought. *You have nothing to lose, it seems, but the threatening bonds of slavery.* There *has* to be another way.

I looked up to see that Heleb was moving to one side. His gun was in his belt and he was holding his hands in such a way as to make display of the fact that they were empty, but he was ready for a quick draw.

"I am going to take up a position behind you," purred Amara Guur. "You will be my shield. Do not turn to look at me—keep perfectly still and be silent. If you move or speak, you die. I think you know that I mean what I say."

"I know," I replied very quietly as I stood up. I risked one quick glance from side to side, without meeting Guur's eye. There was no sign of the other two vormyr.

Ahead of me, I could see Jacinthe Siani and the star-captain approaching. The star-captain was alone. She also seemed to be unarmed. If so, then she was trustingly walking straight into the jaws of a deadly trap.

31

"Where are the others?" asked Guur.

The star-captain didn't answer immediately. Her cold blue eyes were measuring me from head to toe.

"Hello, Trooper Rousseau," she said. "Have you changed sides?" Then, to Guur, she said, "The others will stay where they are, for the time being. I came along to find out what you have to say. They're expecting me to return fairly soon."

"It's simple enough," said Guur. "There's no reason for us to fight. I suggest that we form an alliance. We're all in the same predicament—it may be easier for us to discover a way out if we act in concert."

"That sounds sensible enough," answered Susarma Lear, hands on hips. She gave Heleb a long, considered look. He was standing away to her left. There was nothing between them to obstruct a clear shot. Jacinthe Siani had moved the other way, and was still edging round to be close to Guur. By the sound of his voice, I judged that Guur was directly behind me, with no more than a meter separating us.

"You've got a gun in your hand," observed the star-captain. "That's unfriendly—and unnecessary." She favored me with the briefest of glances as she said it, to indicate the information was meant for me.

"A precaution," said Guur. "There remains one problem, I think. The man named Myrlin. He is dangerous and cannot be trusted. I suggest that he be eliminated."

"I've no objection," drawled the star-captain. "What about *him?*"

She was pointing at me.

"What about him?" countered Guur.

"He's a deserter," she replied. "He's under sentence of death. I think the sentence ought to be carried out."

I began to feel nauseated, but also puzzled. Her tone was all wrong. She was speaking lazily—there was no trace of the sharp, clipped syllables of her normal speech. It wasn't simply that she was using *parole* rather than English. It was deliberate, and there could be only one thing that she was trying to signal by it.

Somewhere back in the bushes, I heard the sound of a crash-gun going off. I didn't waste time hesitating. Guur was right-handed, so I wheeled to the left. I fell sideways, and used my left arm as a lever to pivot my body as I swung both legs backwards. In normal gravity I'd have ended up an ungainly tangled heap on the floor. In one-quarter gravity, the crazy move turned into a somersault that sent me crashing feet first into Amara Guur's chest.

He went flying. He'd already fired the needler, of course, but he'd fired past me at Susarma Lear. Heleb, too, had fired at her, but she was no longer there. He'd expected her to duck, and had aimed low, but she, too, knew something about low gravity tactics, and she'd jumped. I saw her coming down at him, with a flame-gun in her hand that she'd produced from behind her back. The jump was so slow he could have shot her, but his was a crash-gun rather than a beam-weapon, and the recoil had bowled him over—the kinetic energy of the recoil was the same as always, but he weighed far less, and the discrepancy had taken him by surprise.

I couldn't see any more of the captain's fight, because I had to give all my attention to my own. Guur tumbled, but he didn't let go of the needler, and I knew I couldn't give him a second shot. I landed right, and dived forward to tackle him, aiming my shoulder for his gut and my groping hands for his wrist. I got enough of a grip to send the needle well wide, but then he slapped at me with his free hand, hitting me at the side of the neck. It hurt, but the main effect was simply to send us tumbling. He'd been in space, of course, and had some experience of living in no-g, but he hadn't the first idea of how to adapt his fighting style to present circumstances. His reflexes betrayed him all the way along the line.

I took the needler off him, knocked him flying, and pumped half a dozen needles into the bastard's chest. He began to bleed. Profusely.

I looked around, breathing hard. Heleb was flat on his back with a great big cauterized hole in his chest. Susarma Lear was covering Jacinthe Siani, who looked sick. Serne came bouncing out of the bushes with Khalekhan behind him. They were both unscathed.

Serne looked around, spat on the ground, and said: "Amateurs."

"The predator is clever," I murmured. "The predator deceives."

"What was that, Rousseau?" asked the star-captain. Her voice was back to normal.

"Just a little motto I picked up," I said.

"You ran out on us, you bastard," observed Serne.

"That's all right," said the star-captain, collecting Heleb's gun. "We can charge him later, back aboard the ship. These things have to be done according to the regulations." She eyed me speculatively, and said: "You tidied him up pretty well. I thought I might have to get him."

"It was nice of you to try to convince him I was no good to him," I said. "He might have shot me down if you hadn't suggested to him that I was no longer part of the team."

"You may be a lump of shit," she said icily, "but you're a lump of shit *in my command*. I don't forget that—see that *you* remember it from now on."

Gratitude is a wonderful thing, but I wasn't about to let it turn me into a dedicated starship trooper. Diplomacy, however, prevented me from mentioning this fact to my superior officer.

Khalekhan, who had taken over the job of covering Jacinthe Siani, said: "What do we do with *her*?"

"Can't trust her," opined Serne. "Kill her."

"Now just a minute . . ." I began. I had reasons for wanting Jacinthe Siani kept alive.

"Shut up," said Susarma Lear. "You too, Serne. You're big boys, now. No need to be afraid of the girl. She isn't going to give us any trouble—are you?"

Jacinthe Siani spread her arms wide. "What would I have to gain?" she asked. "I'm with you, now." Her voice was hard and assured. She certainly had recovered swiftly from the effects of the sudden turnabout. She gave the impression of being someone who could change sides as easily as she changed her clothes. I was surely keeping company with a lot of nice people these days.

"What about the android?" asked Khalekhan.

"He can't be far away," said the star-captain. "Now we can give him our fullest attention—and if I'm right about this god-damned wall there's no way he can get away from us. We're practically home and dry."

"Oh, Jesus!" I said. "We're only stuck in a bloody cage thousands of kilometers beneath the surface of an alien world, without helmets. *Home and dry!*"

"We're about to finish the job we set out to do," said the blue-eyed captain, radiating fanaticism. "That's what matters, for now. We can think about getting ourselves out when we've done our job. That's the star-force way."

I groaned—discreetly, of course.

The star-captain thrust Heleb's crash-gun into my hand, and said, "Your job is to keep an eye on the prisoner. *Don't* do anything stupid, and if you have to fire that thing, watch out for the recoil."

I looked up at the light-beribboned sky. *You are getting all this, I suppose?* I said, inside my head. *If you need anything explained, you only have to ask. It'd be terrible if you were to miss any of the subtleties for want of a decent commentary.*

As flies to wanton boys, are we to the gods. But they don't have to kill us for their sport. We do it for them.

And then again, to show my versatility:

C'est la guerre, mais ce n'est pas magnifique.

"Rousseau," said the star-captain, as she prepared to move off, "I want you to stay here with the girl. If the corpses worry you, you can move along a little way. Otherwise, don't move until we get back. If by any chance the android finds you before we find him, kill him. That's an order."

I didn't say a word.

32

"As a matter of interest," I said, "how, exactly, did one man manage to kill seven of Amara Guur's thugs and spring Saul Lyndrach?"

She looked me up and down, trying to be contemptuous. Her

obvious uncertainty lessened the effect somewhat. After a brief
interval, she shrugged.

"When Heleb and the others hit Lyndrach's apartment they
found the other one asleep there. They pumped a couple of
darts into him and brought him along. It was a stupid mistake.
He was locked up in a back room while the vormyr went to
work on Lyndrach. He was quiet enough during the day, but he
just bided his time. He tore the door right out and started rip-
ping the place apart. He just smashed them up like rag dolls.
So Heleb says—he was the only one that got out."

Even a Spirellan, it seemed, knew when it came time to drop
his pose. So much for honor and status.

"You'd already fitted me up by then. It was two days *after*
my trial when Myrlin broke out. Why'd you frame me while
you still had Saul?"

She shrugged again. "Insurance," she said. "Once we knew
for sure that you could cope with the language in the notebook,
it made sense to put you on one side."

"Leave nothing to chance," I said, with heavy irony. "Keep
everything neat and tidy. But you didn't quite manage to tidy
up the star-force, did you?"

For once, I think my barbarously intoned *parole* was adequate to carry the message.

"What now?" I asked her, after a pause.

"For the moment," she said, "that depends on you. Then—
even your trigger-happy friends don't count for much really, do
they?"

"I have trigger-happy friends?" I murmured. "That's only because you've run out."

"Are we ever going to get out of here?" she asked, changing
tack.

"I wish I knew," I answered.

Suddenly, somebody switched off the sky. There was a moment of total darkness, and I heard Jacinthe Siani inhale
sharply, almost sobbing with the shock. But she caught and
held the breath as the light came back again; not the bright
pseudo-daylight but a much dimmer, redder light.

I came quickly to my feet, and so did she, swaying as she
tried to correct her reflexive movement to cope with the light
gravity. I looked up at the patterned sky, where the snaky fila-

ments of radiance were moving and flickering. The intensity of the light was no longer sufficient to dazzle, but the shifting of the pattern confused my mind and made me want to turn away. I felt nauseated, and couldn't collect my thoughts. I shielded my eyes with my right arm, but found as I did so that it was no longer necessary. The pattern stabilized again. It was as if the tiny world had been given over to the grip of quiet dusk.

Lowering my arm, I said, "What the hell was *that* all about?"

She didn't answer. She was standing there, still as a statue. I stared at her for a moment then waved my hand in front of her eyes. There was no response.

I hesitated, then poked her shoulder with my forefinger. It wasn't a hard jab, but it was enough to topple her over. She just collapsed, like a puppet whose strings had been cut.

I stood over her, completely at a loss. I looked down at her, up at the mysterious sky, and then out into the shadowed trees. I stood in silence, straining my ears until, at last, I caught a faint sound. I listened while it grew louder. It was the sound of someone approaching with steady, measured tread, rustling the undergrowth as he (or she?) came.

I looked down at the crash-gun, then deliberately threw it aside. I was resigning from *that* league—maybe for good.

I actually breathed a sigh of relief when I saw the size of the shadow that came from the trees, despite the fact that it was of monstrous proportions. It was light enough to see long before he got to me that he was carrying something; in fact, several somethings. I shook my head in wonderment.

It was the first time I'd got a good look at his face. The features were rugged, but by no means unpleasant. He was almost baby-faced—a great big gentle kid.

He dropped the bodies in front of me. Serne, Khalekhan, Susarma Lear—one, two, three. Just like that.

"Dead?" I asked.

Myrlin shook his head. "Merely sleeping."

"Okay," I said. "I give in. How did you do it?"

"I cheated," he replied. "In fact, I didn't do it at all. *They* did." He pointed upward, at the deceptive sky.

I glanced at Jacinthe Siani. "Posthypnotic suggestion," I

said, just to show off how clever I was. "Very spectacular. Real showmen, hey? I take it that you have influence up there?"

"They didn't believe me," he said.

"What didn't they believe?"

"That if they woke you all up, the only thought in your heads would be how and how quickly you could massacre one another."

"No imagination," I said.

"They don't do any killing," he told me. "They don't do much dying, either. They gave it up, a long time ago."

"Really?"

His expression was sober and his voice dead calm. There was a new remoteness in his manner that gave me the impression that I was no longer talking to the same person that I'd been with when I found the city. Of course, it might just have been the fact that we were talking face to face now, without the benefit of a radio link.

"They gave up other things, too," he said. "They gave up reproduction, in the sense that you'd mean it. They abolished sex. They build their children—or maybe I should say 'successors.' They rebuild themselves, too. Technological reincarnation, of a sort. They're biotech minded."

"So I'd heard," I muttered. I didn't feel up to a more substantial contribution, just for the moment, but I managed to take the top one of my long list of questions: "How d'you know?"

"They fed me their language. Same way I was fed the other languages I have . . . not to mention what passes for my identity. In a weird kind of way, I suppose I'm kindred. Maybe that's why they picked me. Maybe I was just lucky."

"Lucky?"

"I just joined the immortals, Mr. Rousseau."

"You can call me Mike," I croaked.

Myrlin pointed at the unconscious starship troopers. "When they wake up," he said, "they're going to remember killing me. As far as they're concerned, they shot me down like a dog. I suppose they'll feel pretty pleased about it."

"They can do that, huh?"

"They could send you back with any memories they cared to

pump into you. They could send you back with any identity they cared to."

"Okay," I said, "I'll bite. What am I going as?"

"You don't have to worry," he said. "You'll remember everything that happened—and nothing that didn't. Otherwise this would be a waste of breath. You can even tell the star-captain that she didn't kill me at all, if you wish. She'll never believe you. She knows different."

"I suppose I ought to thank you for that," I said.

He shook his head.

"I suppose they *are* the builders?" I asked.

Again, he shook his head. "I don't think so. They're exploring, after their fashion, but they've acquired a lot of patience. They know more or less what's in a couple of thousand systems in eight or nine hundred levels; they're in touch with a few hundred other cultures—but they don't know what's in the center any more than we do, Mike. As for the surface . . . they didn't know there *was* a surface. Can you figure that? They thought the levels went on *ad infinitum.* They thought the whole universe was made up of habitable spherical shells. They've got quite a lot of rethinking to do. They need time. You're not going to find them again, Mike. You can have Saul Lyndrach's dropshaft and all the levels that gives you access to. Those are levels *my* people have no particular interest in at present. But you'll never get down here again. No one will, in your lifetime or a hundred like it. My people will make contact again in their own time and on their own terms, when they've decided what to do about the universe."

When they've decided what to do about the universe, I thought. *Just like that—they discover that creation is mostly empty, and that not everybody lives in caves, and so they have to think about how to handle it.*

"They could get to the center if they wanted to," I said. "It can't be more than a couple of thousand kilometers under their feet. Aren't they curious?"

"I don't know," said Myrlin. "I suppose they've tried. Maybe nobody ever gets to the center, Mike. Maybe nobody ever can. I think there are more levels than we imagine . . . more than we *can* imagine . . . and I don't just mean floors and ceilings."

I ducked out of that one. After a pause, I said, "If they

reproduce entirely by means of biotechnology, that makes them androids, doesn't it?" I nearly added: not *real* people at all; but I thought better of it.

"You can create a man who can reproduce, as you would say, *naturally*. A natural man, on the other hand, can grow his successors in an iron womb. An android is a man . . . the difference counts for nothing."

"What about the people of the city?" I asked.

"Redundant android servitors, expelled by some culture several hundred levels up from here, but still maintained in their half-life. A twisted kind of conscience, perhaps, but conscience nevertheless."

"But you're going to cut them off. You're going to leave us our access to that level, but seal off the lower ones. What happens to them *then*?"

"Then," he said, calmly, "they're on someone else's conscience, aren't they? You come into the levels hunting for loot and not for responsibilities—you and all your kind—but you can't always rely on finding what you want, can you?"

"Did Asgard come from the black galaxy?" I asked, realizing even as I did so what the answer must be.

"How could we know where Asgard came from, or where it is going, or why?"

My people, I thought. *How could we know . . . ?*

I looked around slowly at all the silent bodies, dead and unconscious . . . at the giant android who was now more alien than even his makers had intended him to be . . . at the trees where the shadows gathered in crowds to hoard their secrets . . . at the patterned sky, servant of the whims of an unseen, unknown people.

"So this is what it all comes to?" I asked him, rhetorically.

"This is it," he confirmed. "One small experiment, and one specimen retained. I hope that you appreciate the irony of the fact that the informant who will teach them what they want to know about the universe . . . and about the human race and its neighbors . . . should be an unnatural creature who came by all that knowledge dishonestly. I think you do. From my point of view, remember, there's a sense in which I'm coming home. For me, if not for you, it's very neat and proper."

I gestured with my right hand. "I don't begrudge you that,"

I said. "I'll settle for what I have. It's enough, and maybe more than enough."

He raised his own hand, but not to make a dismissive gesture. He was holding a mindscrambler.

"Just one more thing," I said quickly.

He paused and waited.

"Thanks," I said wryly, "for the memory."

"And that's more or less it," I said, recrossing my ankles and accidentally knocking a stylo off the desk. "There was no trouble when we got back to the surface. The eagle eye of the peace officers was upon us, and Jacinthe Siani had warned the guys in Guur's trucks that their operation was a loser all along the line. Jacinthe's in jail now, of course. She's confessed to more or less everything, including the big frame-up. I'm being retried in a couple of hours, and will be completely exonerated. Among other things, that invalidates the conscription papers which I signed under duress. My brief and spectacular career as a starship trooper comes to an end. I daresay the star-captain won't be pleased, but I'll try to lessen the blow by pointing out that conscription or no conscription, there's no way the inhabitants of Skychain City would let her spirit me away into the depths of space. I'm *far* too valuable, aren't I?"

Aleksandr Sovorov was staring at me as if I were some kind of hairy arthropod with a disgusting odor. It wasn't just the fact that I had my feet on his desk, either. The account I'd given him of my adventures in the underworld had been heavily censored, of course, but the meat of it was all there.

"You're telling me," he said slowly, "that you actually made contact with an advanced culture based a thousand levels down."

"More, probably," I said. "I never got an exact figure, or even a near estimate."

"And that because of what they learned from you and from the assorted thugs you took with you, these people have sealed off the levels under their influence for an indeterminate period?"

"They seemed to think that we're uncivilized," I said, ramming the point home with delicate understatement. "But then, so does everybody else. Maybe they're right."

He groaned. He always was a big ham. "Do you have any conception of what you've *done?*" he asked, practically bugeyed with resentful fury.

"Yes," I said, goading him a bit further. "I've opened up a lot of new levels. I've found the dropshaft that gives us access to a surface area greater than fifty Earth-size planets. I'm a hero. And I've done myself a bit of good, too, because of all the ones who made it back, I'm the only one who has the memory and the know-how to find my way back."

"You *stupid,* selfish *bastard,*" he said, practically hissing the words through his teeth. "You may have lost the human race and all its neighbor races the greatest opportunity that will come to them in centuries, and you have the nerve to feel *smug!*"

I think he might cheerfully have murdered me—if it hadn't been for the fact that he was trying *so* hard to be a civilized man (unlike me), and for the fact that I was still the only man who could give the C.R.E. access to those lower levels. It was time, though, for the *coup de grace.*

I picked up a piece of notepaper from his desk and pointed to the letterhead.

"What's that, Alex?" I asked.

I had to wait for him to cool down enough to respond sensibly. Eventually, he was able to look where I was pointing.

"That's a pictograph in the Tetron language," he said. "It's the name of our organization. Much neater to put it in a single symbol than to spell it out in phonetic *parole.* Why?"

"It appears on all your documents—a kind of trademark?"

"Yes. So what?"

"That's the symbol Myrlin drew in the air when he told me about the Salamandrans buying biotechnics from Asgard. Your beloved Coordinated Research Establishment has been bootlegging technics to be used in biological warfare. If things had gone as scheduled, the human race would be facing the future with a self-confidence that would be less than warranted. Your friends, Alex, damn near contrived the genocide of your own species, and you helped them. So who's civilized, Alex? How real is the harmonious cooperation within your magnificent organization? And who's being taken for a ride by a bunch of biotech-minded con men?"

"You're lying," he said, in a tone too flat to be hopeful.

I shook my head.

"I didn't know," he said eventually. "I didn't know *anything*. . . ."

"I know *that*," I reassured him. "That's why I thought I ought to bring you up to date. All the news that's fit to print . . . and some that isn't."

He thought about it for a minute, and then said, "It doesn't in the least affect my condemnation of you. I stand by everything I believe. What you've contrived is a disaster for humankind, and for humanoid civilization throughout known space."

"When you come right down to it, though," I said, "it isn't just me, is it? People in general are pretty disappointing. You can't trust the Tetrax any more than the vormyr. It has to be the Tetrax who derived those technics from the stuff we've scavenged from the levels—hasn't it?"

"Very likely," he admitted.

I left it at that. "You'll be glad to know," I said, "that I've renewed my application to the C.R.E. for a grant to help me carry on my independent investigations down below. This time, I think the powers that be will grant it, with or without your recommendation." I stood up and raised my hand in a salute of farewell.

He looked astonished. "After finding *that* out," he said, "You're still going to deal with C.R.E.?"

"Sure," I said. "It may be a crooked game—but there ain't no honest ones in *this* town."

"You aren't expecting me to resign?"

"Hell, no," I said. "I like to have a friend on the inside. Especially one who makes a special effort to keep track of what's going on."

I think he got the message.

The next stop on my schedule was the courtroom. I got there in good time, and sat through the whole retrial, which lasted about a unit and a half, SMT. The star-captain was there too, and she didn't turn a hair when the conscription papers I'd signed were declared null and void. In fact, she seemed to be in a fairly good temper. Things might have been different, I guess, if she'd known that Myrlin was still alive and well. Nobody knew that except me, and nobody was going to know. I'd been vague so far about the source of the information I'd received from him in that final interview, and I was prepared to keep on being mysterious until I died. An air of mystery gives a guy that certain *je ne sais quoi.*

Afterward, I walked back to the skychain with Susarma Lear.

"You got out of this very nicely, didn't you?" she said.

"Fair to middling," I confessed.

"You'd have saved us a lot of trouble if you'd taken that android in when Immigration Control asked you to," she observed. "A lack of charity is a terrible thing."

"Sure," I said. "You'd have got the android without any fuss —maybe. I'd have ended up wound tight in Amara Guur's little spiderweb—maybe. I can live with my conscience if you can live with yours."

"I could have made a Trooper out of you," she said regretfully. "I really could."

"Before or after you had me shot for desertion?"

"Instead of," she assured me.

"You want to know what really gets me?" I said. "About you?"

"You're kinky for girls in uniform," she countered coldly.

"The fact that you're going back up the chain without a twinge of regret," I told her. "Except perhaps about not being able to work your evil way with my independent spirit. You really don't care, do you—about what we found down there? It all means nothing to you: the levels; the center; the immortal biotechnicians. You don't give a damn."

"I have a job to do," she told me in return. "It's a matter of duty. That's the star-force way."

"I know," I said. And again, for emphasis: "I know."

I didn't suppose that I'd ever see her again, and for that fateful mercy I thanked whatever gods there might be, above or below.

As I walked home, I brooded on the only two worries I had

left. They were private worries, that I'd never be able to share with anyone else.

The first was to do with the Salamandrans, and the untrustworthiness of appearances. It ran like this. Suppose they *had* been able to bring their genetic time-bomb project to a successful conclusion, but were worried about security. Suppose that they figured there was no way they could keep the dread secret from leaking out in the course of the next couple of centuries. They could cover their own tracks well enough, no doubt—but they couldn't cover up the C.R.E. end of the operation, and probably didn't dare to try. So what recourse would they have, except to try a really cunning false trail trick? Maybe they thought their best chance was to let the conquering humans find out about the project, but to let them believe that it was dead and dealt with. Everything Myrlin had told me might be as straight as a die, and the conclusion that the human race was in no danger whatsoever might be strictly on the level—but how could I, or anyone else, ever really be certain?

The problem is, you see, that Myrlin knew only what they pumped into him—nothing more and nothing less. Who knows how dependable he was?

And that, of course, was the pointer to my second, more personal worry, which was that I was in much the same boat. Once having accepted that the underworlders could play with people's memories exactly as they wished—and the star-captain's conviction that she had shot Myrlin was presumably proof of the fact—how could I be certain that what *I* remembered was really true? How could I know whether Myrlin's last promise was sound, or whether the promise itself was a false memory implanted in me by just the same means that the star-captain had acquired her fond memories of android-murder. There was no way, really, that I could be sure of *anything* that had happened to me after I was first hit by the mindscrambler —and I might be wrong even about things that had happened before. It was conceivable that Myrlin *was* dead, and that the race of immortal biotechnicians was just a flimsy fantasy thrown into my head by some other kind of critter entirely.

They were two insoluble problems. I didn't know the answer to either of them, and I never would. My instinct was to trust my judgment that the Salamandran project *had* failed and that M14 what I remembered about the world far below *was* true . . . but we all know what happens to people who put too much trust in their instincts. Look at Amara Guur, to name but one. In the end, I decided to accept the apparent truth as the genuine article. There's nothing to be gained from constantly puzzling over the insoluble. In the famous last words of one of the most profound philosophical documents ever penned by a human hand, *il faut cultiver notre jardin.*

At least, in Asgard, I had the biggest bloody *jardin* in the known universe.

Or, to put it another way, what Myrlin said is probably true. We never will reach the Center, because we never can. That pure, unadulterated kernel of Absolute Certainty is forever out of reach, and when it comes to the end of the day, you have to settle for what you can get.